Beiträge zur Indologie

Herausgegeben von Konrad Meisig

Begründet von Ulrich Schneider als
Freiburger Beiträge zur Indologie

Band 54

2025
Harrassowitz Verlag · Wiesbaden

Konrad Meisig

The Yogasūtras of Patañjali

Sanskrit and English
A New Translation Based on Textual Criticism

2025
Harrassowitz Verlag · Wiesbaden

Bibliografische Information der Deutschen Nationalbibliothek
Die Deutsche Nationalbibliothek verzeichnet diese Publikation in der Deutschen Nationalbibliografie; detaillierte bibliografische Daten sind im Internet über https://dnb.dnb.de abrufbar.

Bibliographic information published by the Deutsche Nationalbibliothek
The Deutsche Nationalbibliothek lists this publication in the Deutsche Nationalbibliografie; detailed bibliographic data are available in the internet at https://dnb.dnb.de.

For further information about our publishing program consult our website https://www.harrassowitz-verlag.de

Kreuzberger Ring 7c-d, 65205 Wiesbaden, produktsicherheit.verlag@harrassowitz.de

Printed on permanent/durable paper.
Printing and binding: Prime Rate, Budapest
Printed in Hungary

ISSN 1432-6949
ISBN 978-3-447-12438-6
eISBN 978-3-447-39729-2

Content

Patañjali's Urtext and the Formation of the Yogasūtras: Textual Criticism

Postscript

Patañjali's Urtext and the Formation of the Yogasūtras: Textual Criticism

The Yogasūtras shall be analysed here according to the method of historical textual criticism. It is divided in four branches thus created, in criticism of:

- text witnesses
- content
- stylistic forms
- redactions

Criticism of the Text Witnesses

The text of the Yogasūtras[1] is almost uniformly handed down in a couple of authoritative current editions. These served as the basis of my *Yogasūtra-Konkordanz* (1988). The resulting text is what one may call, in analogy to the biblical exegesis, a vulgate (the generally accepted version of a text).

Of course one could endeavour to collect the most ancient manuscripts available to constitute an archetype, following Paul Maas' *Textual Criticism* (1967). I refrained from doing so for two reasons.

Firstly, a classical scripture like the Yogasūtras can be found in thousands of manuscripts spread all over India and abroad. This would have been a large-scale research project, going beyond my organisational limits.

Secondly, there is, still today, a wide-spread and lively oral tradition that continuously contaminates the systematic dependence of the written witnesses. Therefore, the following text-critical steps are restricted to the vulgate.

Criticism of the Content

The text of the vulgate is traditionally divided into four 'chapters.' The criticism of the content (also called literary criticism) will start with a simple rearrangement of these four chapters as follows:

1 Sanskrit basic text with concordance can be found in the author's: *Yogasûtra-Konkordanz*, 1988. The basic text with the commentary of Vyāsa and an English translation of both gives Bangali Baba: *Yogasûtra of Patañjali*, 1976. See also the bibliography of Yoga by P. Schreiner: *Yoga. Grundlagen, Methoden, Ziele. Ein bibliographischer Überblick*, 1979.

Vulgate text of the Yogasūtras (=YS):
'Chapters' One – Two – Three – Four

These four chapters correspond roughly with my rearranged:
Parts B – P – C – D.

So 'Chapter' One corresponds roughly with my Part B, 'Chapter' Two with Part P, 'Chapter' Three with Part C, and 'Chapter' Four with Part D.

P is the abbreviation for Patañjali. P is the most ancient part of the vulgate. Part B, although it appears today as 'Chapter' One of the Yogasūtras, is nothing but a later addition to Patañjali's earliest text P. Therefore I have rearranged the sūtras according to their historical order:

Parts	§	P –	B –	C –	D	(+ E)
Chapters	YS	Two –	One –	Three –	Four	

My extra Part E contains all the 'extras' (i.e. the minor interpolations) which were added in later phases of the text formation and are scattered all over the 'Chapters' One and Two of the Vulgate.[2]

This rearrangement, according to the historical and logical order, is based on the fact that the text of the vulgate contains a significant number of repetitions, contradictions and dislocations. They can be explained by the following presumptions:

The author of the nucleus or core of the Yogasūtras is actually unknown, in terms of being an historical figure. The Indian tradition calls him Patañjali. But this Patañjali is not a verifiable individual. He – or it – is a process of oral recitation. For reasons of simplicity, however, I will continue to call these early recitations by the personal name of Patañjali.[3]

What was recited was a corpus of meditation maxims, called sūtra. A sūtra, literally a 'thread,' is a short rule or maxim[4] in prose, serving as an aide-mémoire. It is the ambition of an author of a sūtra to say as much as possible with as few words as possible.

The objective of the criticism of content is to reconstruct the content of this earliest corpus of oral recitations.

2 My parts P-E are numbered in paragraphs (§) according to the logical content. In order to facilitate the orientation for the reader, I usually quote the paragraph number first, but also add the traditional number of the respective sūtra in brackets, e. g. '§ B41 (=YS 1,41).'

3 The meaning of this name might be 'Bird,' but this is very doubtful. *patañjali* could be a prakritism for *patañ-cala*, which would be a 'spur-of-the-moment-formation' after *pataṅ-ga*, according to J. Przyluski, see: Wackernagel/Debrunner (Alt.ind. Gram., I, Nachtr. 64) and Mayrhofer (Etym. WB).

4 A maxim is 'a short statement expressing a general truth or rule of behaviour.' Aphorism would be the wrong word. An aphorism is 'a short witty remark which contains a general truth.' Neither does 'mnemonic' hit the point, as not all Yogasūtras 'follow a pattern of letters or words.' (The definitions are quoted from the *Oxford Dictionary Thesaurus*, 2001.)

In written tradition, the initial draft, personally inscribed or jotted down by the author, is called the 'original.' Of course such an original of the Yogasūtras has not been passed down to us. The second best version, nearest to an 'original,' would be a copy of the origininal. In many other instances, this is the earliest text version that can be reconstructed on the basis of historically sound and reliable manuscripts. It would be called the 'archetype,' and, in the absence of appropriate manuscripts, we also cannot reconstruct such an 'archetype' of the Yogasūtras.

What we can reconstruct is the content of the earliest oral tradition, forming the nucleus of the vulgate. It is not the 'original,' neither is it the 'archetype.' I call this underlying, *core of orally recited maxims*, the '*urtext.*'

When and where this oral urtext was first written down, we do not know.[5]

The wording of the urtext, of what 'Patañjali composed,' is submerged under secondary, accidental, ancillary tendencies made by later adaptors, reworkers and revisors. The text of the vulgate (abbreviated YS) must therefore be judged as the product of a historical development. In the course of centuries, there were not only one, but several anonymous authors in succession. These editors modified the wording according to their own wide-spread preferences. Their manipulations resulted in interpolations (i.e. additions) and dislocations (misplacements). Not only words and single sūtras had been added and misplaced, but even whole passages of paragraphs.

The method of internal literary criticism is used to reconstruct a text previous to the state in which it is handed down to us. This restoration does not need to rely on the commentary of Vyāsa.[6] It actually treats the vulgate as a closed circuit. The examination of irregularities, like repetitions, contradictions and dislocations will result in establishing the genealogical tree (stemma) of the historical formation of the vulgate, the Yogasūtras in their growth and development from 'Patañjali's' urtext down to the modern editions.

Criticism of Stylistic Forms

Criticism of stylistic forms can provide additional proof for the validity of the results of the former two branches of textual criticism (of the text witnesses and of the content). In the case of the Yogasūtras, however, its possibilities are rather restricted. A sūtra *is* already a stylistic form, it is *the* short form of classical Sanskrit literature (the *sūtra* is a genre in prose, as opposed to the metrical *kārikā*, for example the Sāṃkhyakārikās).

5 More fortunate, by the way, is the situation in the case of the Buddhist Pāli canon. It was written down for the first time in Ceylon in the years 89-77 BC, about one hundred years after Patañjali.

6 Vyāsa dates from about six centuries later than the sūtras. There is no indication of an uninterrupted text tradition from the urtext to Vyāsa over this lengthy period of time. To the contrary, all evidence points in the direction of Vyāsa having an encyclopaedic knowledge of the yoga movements of his era (~ 500 AD), but did not have any intention of understanding the sūtras in a historical perspective.

Of course, the form always depends on the content. But if we are prepared to tolerate the blending of mould and meaning, we can discern different varieties of sūtras:

There are sūtras in the form of

• the philosophical theorem, like:

draṣṭṛ-dṛśyayoḥ saṃyogo heya-hetuḥ.
The conjunction of soul and matter
is the basic obstacle which must be abandoned.
(§ P1)

The same stylistic form, the philosophical theorem, also occurs at § (P1) P5 P29 B2 B3 B41 C43 C48 and D1.

Another stylistic form is the more detailed:

• philosophical explication:

duḥkha-daurmanasyâṅgamejayatva-śvāsa-praśvāsā vikṣepa-sahabhuvaḥ.
Suffering, moroseness, tremor of the limbs and heavy breathing
are the symptoms of the distractions.
(§ B31)

This very common stylistic form occurs also at § P2 P3 P4 P6 P7 P8 P9 B4 B5 B8 B9 B10 B11 B13 B14 B15 B18 B19 B20 B24 B26 B29 B40 C44 C47 D2 D3 D4 D6 D7 D9 D10 D12 D14 D15 D16 D17 D18 D19 D24 E3 E7 E19 E29 E31 E37 E38.

There are sūtras transporting a:

• non-philosophical comment:

jāti-deśa-kāla-samayânavacchinnāḥ sārva-bhaumā mahāvratam.
Because these moral prohibitions are independent of the kind of birth (or: caste),
country, time and moment, and because they extend to all levels,
they constitute a grand vow.
(§ P15)

They are to be found at § P23 P26 C30 C39 E6 E9 E10 E11 E12 E13 E14 and E41.

Sūtras containing:

• practical advice for meditation are very frequent, like:

sthira-sukham āsanam.
A firm and comfortable sitting posture.
(§ P 32)

Also at P17 P18 P19 P20 P21 P22 P24 P25 P27 P28 C01 C03 C04 C05 B32 B33 B34 B35 B36 B37 B38 B39 C28 C45 C46 D13 D21 D25 D28 D29 D30 D31 D32 D33 E4 E21 E22 E32 E33 E34 E35 E36 E40.

The following are aide-mémoires which are meant to be kept in mind during a continuous period of meditational exercises. I call them:

• the reminders:

viveka-khyātir aviplavā hānôpāyaḥ.
Continuous perception of the difference is the means of abandoning.
(P10)

§ P10 P11 P12 B27 B28.

There are a couple of sūtras with a:

• mnemotechnical enumeration:

yama-niyamâsana-prāṇāyāma-pratyāhāra-dhāraṇā-dhyāna-samādhayo 'ṣṭāv aṅgāni.
The eight members are morality, self-discipline, sitting posture, breath control, drawing back the sense organs, steadying the thinking, meditation and 'concentration.'
(§ P13)

§ P13 P14 P16 B6 B7 B12 B30 B31 C39? E2? E20.

• the psycho-analytical diagnosis:
(Sūtras containing this stylistic form sometimes overlap with the philosophical explication.)

vyutthāna-nirodha-saṃskārayor abhibhava-prādurbhāvau nirodha-kṣaṇa-cittânvayo nirodha-pariṇāmaḥ.
The overpowering of the imprint of activity
and the appearance of the imprint of the shutdown
are its transformation.
It follows the thinking in the moment of its shutdown.
(§ C1)

B16 B17 C1 C2 C3 C4 C5 C6 C7 C10 C12 C36 D5 D8 D11 D26 D27 E17 E18 E39 E40.

Yet other stylistic forms are:

• the magical or parapsychological instruction:

pariṇāma-traya-saṃyamād atītânāgata-jñānam.
From the 'interconnection' of the triad of transformation
comes the recognition of past and future.
(§ C8)

§ B21 B22 B23 C02 C03 C05 C8 C9 C10 C11 (related to C27 and D20) C13 C14 C15 C16 C17 C18 C19 C20 C21 C22 C23 C24 C25 C29 C31 C32 C33 C34 C35 C37 C38 C40 C41 C42 D20 D22 D23 E30.

• the sermon:

sa pūrveṣām api guruḥ kālenânavacchedāt.
'He (*īśvara*) was the teacher of the ancients too, owing to his timelessness.'

(§ E26)

E15 E16 E23 E24 E25 E26 E27 E28.

• the spell (*mantra*):

viśokā jyotiṣmatī!
Exemption from grief, possessed with light!
(§ B36), or:

prātibhāt sarvam!
Enlightenment brings everything!
(C26)

• the proverbial saying:

heyaṃ duḥkham anāgatam.
One must get rid of future suffering.
(§ B25), or:

asteya-pratiṣṭhāyāṃ sarva-ratnôpasthānam.
On the basis of 'not stealing' all jewels assemble.
(§ E8)

• the simile (*upamā*):

kṣīṇa-vṛtter abhijātasyêva maṇer...
...as in the case of a classy jewel...
(§ B41)

All other instances with the particle *iva* ('similar to' or 'as it were') are → paradoxa.

• the exaggeration.
The Sanskrit poetology (Alaṃkāraśāstra) knows this figure of speech as *atiśaya*, which means just 'exaggeration':

paramâṇu-parama-mahattvânto 'sya vaśīkāraḥ.
His self-discipline ends in the smallest and greatest.
(C26)

§ C26 C42 D22 D30 E8 E30.
And finally, there is:

• the paradox:

asteya-pratiṣṭhāyāṃ sarva-ratnôpasthānam.
On the basis of 'not stealing' all jewels assemble.
(§ E8)

All instances (except B41) with the particle of comparison, *iva*[7], are paradoxical as well. In these cases, categories that virtually can't be compared, are correlated nevertheless, because they share, paradoxically, common properties.[8]

The stylistic forms of the Yogasūtras can help to identify characteristics specific to the personalities of certain scribes, their habits and customs. Occasionally, they even have strong supporting argumentative value. Examples are:

• the cluster of 'non-philosophical comments' in the spurious paragraphs E9-14 (see p. 22);

• the virtual non-existence of the stylistic form of the 'mnemotechnical enumeration' in parts C and D (see p. 5), whereas Patañjali and the imitator show no inhibitions to freely make use of it;

• similarly Pataṇjali in his part P never tries a 'psycho-analytical diagnosis' (see p. 5); nor:

• the 'parapsychological instruction.'

• The 'sermon' only occurs in the theological sūtras (see p. 5).

Criticism of Redactions

I have dealt so far with the first three branches of textual criticism, namely the text witnesses, the content and the stylistic forms. All three methods go back in time. They start with the text that we find in the present and try to reconstruct a previous state, moving backwards. The fourth branch, the criticism of redactions, goes in the opposite direction. It starts at the historical beginnings and pursues the changes and transformations of the text, trying to understand the motives of the respective revisors and their teaching tendencies which led to the formation of the Yogasūtras as we read and hear them today.

The first three branches of textual criticism proceed analytically: the text corpus lies on the table in the dissection room. Criticism of redactions, number four, reassembles the parts and pieces together the fragments – it works synthetically.

The Progenitor: Patañjali
Part P and the Major Eightfold Path

The Yogasūtras, as they are handed down to us, are dominated by two decisive influences. There is, on the one hand, the meditation practice of the yoga schools of the ancient Indian asceticism. And there are, on the other, marked impacts of Buddhism, whose founder, the historical Siddhārtha Gautama (called by his honorary title, the Buddha, the 'Awoken One'), lived about 300 years before Patañjali.

7 Meaning 'as it were', § P25 P29 B15 E32. The suffix *-vat* is used in a simile in § D2, *kṣetrika-vat*, 'like a peasant.'

8 The metaphorology is discussed in detail at § P29, see p. 43.

Both, yoga and Buddhism, shared the desire to end the cycle of rebirth, to bring it to a halt, to dry out – as it were – the eternal maelstrom. And both sought a *rational* kind of redemption.

• The yogic teachers advocated the 'non-existence of ignorance' (*avidyā-abhāva*).[9] The 'law of dependent origin' (*pratītya-samutpāda*) of the canonical Buddhism also starts with 'ignorance' (*avidyā*), considering it to be the original cause of the universal suffering of rebirth.

• The Buddha proclaimed his 'eightfold path' and Patañjali's path comprises 'eight members' as well.[10]

• Yoga and Buddhism cultivated the meditation practice of 'concentration' (*samādhi*) as the appropriate means and final point of their respective ways to deliverance.

• Both share the meditation techniques of mindfulness (*smṛti*),

• friendliness (*maitrī*, Pāli *mettā*),

• and the prime precept of non-violence (*ahiṃsā*).[11]

Equally, they start out from the conviction that 'all is only suffering.' *Duḥkham eva sarvam*, reads the Yogasūtra[12]; *sarvam eva duḥkham* say the Buddhists.

The nucleus of the ancient collection of sūtras is well concealed, embedded in its vulgate covers. But it is clearly characterised by a marked tendency towards rationality. Patañjali has made himself independent from all exterior forces: from social constraints, tradition, gods, magic, or drugs. He decides his own fate by his own deeds. His first deed is to refrain from all deeds, to avoid all kinds of karma, to seek redemption from all suffering of the reincarnation.

Patañjali's teachings are contained in what I call Part P of the Yogasūtras. This Part P is divided into two sections. It starts with the theoretical foundations,[13] which run parallel to the philosophy of the dualistic Sāṃkhya system. From the outset, Patañjali makes it clear that the yogī must abandon the erroneous connection (*saṃyoga*) of matter (*sva*) and soul (*svāmin*) to reach 'isolation' (*kaivalya*), the state of pure 'observing' (*dṛśi*), when the soul observes only itself. In the second section, he teaches the major eightfold path to deliverance. The eight members of this path start with an ascetic moral conduct, continue with a series of meditation exercises, and end with the mental state which is called 'concentration' (*samādhi*), that is concentration of the soul on itself, in other words: of the identification of subject and object.

9 § P9 (= YS 2,25).

10 Both call the constituents of their eightfold path 'members,' *aṅga*: the Buddhists have their *aṣṭâṅgaka-mārga*, the Yogasūtras count *aṣṭāv aṅgāni*, § P13 (=YS 2,29).

11 Mindfulness (*smṛti*) § B11 (=YS 1,11) or § E32 (=YS 1,43), friendliness (*maitrī*) § P18 (=YS 1,33), non-violence (*ahiṃsā*) § E5 (=YS 2,34).

12 § B24 (=YS 2,15).

13 § P1-9 (=YS 2,17-25).

It is obvious that Patañjali has adopted his eightfold path from the Buddhist *aṣṭâṅ-ga-mārga* अष्टाङ्गमार्ग, which is after all 300 years older. The octodus (ὀκτώδος) of the Buddha starts with an ethical conduct, passes through several meditation drills, and finds its conclusion in the state of 'concentration' (*samādhi*).[14] Patañjali has followed this structure.

Patañjali's Eightfold Path to Redemption
8 Constituents
(1) Morality (*yama*), the moral prohibitions Non-violence, truthfulness, not stealing, chastity, not clinging
(2) Self-discipline (*niyama*), the moral precepts Purity and contentedness
(3) Sitting posture (*āsana*)
(4) Breath control (*prāṇāyāma*)
(5) Drawing back the sense organs (*pratyāhāra*)
(6) Steadying the thinking (*dhāraṇā*)
(7) Meditation (*dhyāna*)
(8) Concentration (*samādhi*)

This was the essence and the starting point of systematising the yoga teachings. All remaining parts, the post-Patañjali sūtras, in fact the majority of the text of today's Yogasūtras, are imitations, parallels with heterogeneous terminology, or even contradictory, inconsistent additions and interpolations, which must be strictly kept apart from Patañjali's urtext.

Thus, *Yogasūtra version 1.0.*, Patañjali's urtext, laid the foundations for all later variants. It had the following content:

§ P1-16 (=YS 2,17-32); § P17-26 (=YS 2,46-55); P27-29 (=YS 3,1-3).

The Imitator: Part B and the Minor Eightfold Path

Part B is the work of an imitator who clumsily kept himself to Patañjali's urtext. He awkwardly mimicked Patañjali's approach by placing the theoretical foundations first. He continued with a practical part, as well, with also eight exercises of meditation, which he termed 'clarifications.' They are but a'minor' eightfold path, as opposed to Patañjali's 'major' eightfold path of Part P.

The minor eightfold path is directed towards the 'unification' (*samāpatti*) of the soul. In order to reach this destination, the imitator defines yoga as the 'shutdown of the brain movements.'[15]

14 See U. Schneider: *Der Buddhismus*, 1997^4, pp. 84ff.

15 § B2 (= YS 1,2).

Parts P and B share the same philosophical foundation, namely the dualistic Sāṃkhya system. They just belong to different schools of yoga which teach different mental techniques, using heterogeneous terminologies for the same objects. What has been termed the 'seer'[16] in Part P, namely the soul, is now called the 'receiver'[17] in Part B. Subsequently the 'seeable' (*dṛśya*), the matter, of Part P, now becomes the 'perceivable' (*grāhya*). What has been called *dṛśi*, the process of 'seeing,' in Part P, turns out to be synonymous with *grahaṇa*, the process of 'perceiving' in Part B. As both parts, P and B, are nevertheless closely related to each other, they could easily be combined in one collection or rather a compilation of sūtras.

The minor eightfold path of Part B consists of a number of diverse exercises called 'clarifications' (*prasādana*). It commences with:

(1) the exercise of concentration on one 'real object' (*tattva*),
(2) the meditative creation of friendliness, compassion, pleasure and equanimity,
(3) exhaling or stretching of the breath,
(4) contemplation of an object of sense (*viṣaya*) in a 'solid state of mind,'
(5) contemplation of light (*jyotis*),
(6) contemplation of an 'object of sense' (*viṣaya*) 'without passion' (*vīta-rāga*),
(7) perception dependent from dream and deep sleep, concluded by
(8) 'meditation' (*dhyāna*) on an optional subject.

The following synopsis, a comparison of parts P and B, should make the dependency of the imitator from Patañjali's urtext clearer.

Comparison of Parts P and B

Part P Isolation of the Soul	Part B Unification of the Soul
Theoretical Foundations (§ P1-9)	*Theoretical Foundations* (§ B2-4)
Abandon the conjunction of soul and matter! (§ P1) 'The conjunction has its cause in the false impression that the two potencies, matter and soul, both seem to	Yoga is the Shutdown of the Brain Movements (§ B1-2) 'Then the soul stands apart from that which has the shape of the matter.' (B3) 'Otherwise the soul has the same shape as the brain movements (which are part of the matter).' (B4)

16 *draṣṭṛ*, § P4 (=YS 2,20)

17 *grahītṛ*, § B41 (=YS 1,41).

adopt that which has the shape of the matter.' (P7)	

Part P can be headlined, 'isolation (*kaivalya*) of the soul,' Part B, 'unification of the soul.' Part P begins with theoretical foundations, Part B too. Here Part P starts with the admonition, to 'abandon the conjunction of soul and matter.' Part B defines yoga as 'the shutdown of the brain movements,' so that, 'the soul stands apart from that which has the shape of the matter.' Whereas Part P diagnoses that, 'the conjunction has its cause in the false impression that the two potencies, matter and soul, both seem to adopt that which has the shape of the matter,' Part B notices that, 'otherwise the soul has the same shape as the brain movements (which are part of the matter).'

Attributes of the Matter (§ P2-3) 'The nature of which is brightness, action and firmness, what completely consists of elements and organs of sense, which has as its objective experience and avoidance, that is the matter.'	Movements and Defilements (§ B5) The Brain Movements (§ B6-11) 'The movements are: means of perception, error, imagination, deep sleep and mindfulness.' Defilements of the Thinking (§ B12-25) 'Ignorance, egocentricity, passion, hate and zest for life are the defilements.'

Part P continues to explain the *general* attributes of the matter as being, 'brightness, action and firmness.' Matter, it reads, 'consists completely of elements and organs of sense, having as its objective experience and avoidance.' Part B varies the theme by restricting itself to the *disadvantageous* attributes, the 'movements and defilements': 'The movements are: means of perception, error, imagination, deep sleep and mindfulness,'... 'Ignorance, egocentricity, passion, hate and zest for life are the defilements.'

Attributes of the Soul (§ P4) The Relation between Matter and Soul (§ P5-8)	The Five Defilements in Detail (§ B13-18) Getting Rid of the Defilements (§ B19-20) The Root of the Defilements (§ B21-25)

Part P continues with the attributes of the soul and the relation between matter and soul. Part B runs not quite parallel, because it has to finish its theme by explaining how one gets rid of the defilements.

Isolation (§ P9) 'The non-existence of the conjunction is: the abandoning. This is the isolation.' (P9)	Shutdown by Exercising and Dispassion (§ B26) 'By exercising and dispassion, the shutdown of the movements can be accomplished.' (B26)

The introductory theoretical foundations are again not literally, but similarly ended by returning to the respective statements with which they began. Part P states that 'the non-existence of the conjunction is the abandoning. This is the isolation.' And Part B records that, 'by exercising and dispassion, the shutdown of the movements can be accomplished.'

The Eightfold Path of Yoga (§ P10-29)	*The Minor Eightfold Path, or: The Clarifications* (§ B32-39)
Reminders, and the Eight Constituents (§ P10-13) 'Continuous perception of the difference is the means of abandoning the false impression of the identity of soul and matter.' (P10)	Exercising (§ B27-28) 'And if one has attended to the exercising for a long time without interruption and with care, one's eight steps of the 'clarifications' are firmly founded.' (B28)

After that, both parts move on to their proclamations of their respective eightfold paths, the major one in Part P, which makes a clear and well thought-out impression; and the minor one of Part B, which is an unconvincing, wan ersatz. Even the three reminders of Part P, like: 'Continuous perception of the difference is the means of abandoning the false impression of the identity of soul and matter,' find their parallel by laying stress on the necessity of exercising in Part B: 'And if one has attended to the exercising for a long time without interruption and with care, one's eight steps of the clarifications are firmly founded.'

	Distractions and Clarifications (§ B29-39)
(1) Morality (*yama*), the moral prohibitions (§ P14-15) 'non-violence, truthfulness, not stealing, chastity and not clinging.' (P14)	Distractions (§ B29-31) ~ Distractions of the Thinking (B30): 'Illness, rigour, doubt, carelessness, laziness, worldly attachment, mental confusion, failure (on the path to deliverance) and unsteadiness.' (1) the exercise of contemplation of one 'real object' (*tattva*)

The major eightfold path of Part P starts with (no. 1) morality (*yama*), the moral prohibitions, 'non-violence, truthfulness, not stealing, chastity and not clinging.' The imitator corresponds with what he calls the 'distractions of the thinking,' scil. 'illness, rigour, doubt, carelessness, laziness, worldly attachment, mental confusion, failure on the path to deliverance and unsteadiness,' which is directly followed by his first 'clarification,' (no. 1) the exercise of contemplation of one 'real object.' The wording *eka-tattvâbhyāsaḥ* is modelled after *pratyaya-eka-tānatā dhyānam*, no. 7 of Part P.

(2) Self-Discipline Purity and contentedness (P16)	(2) The meditative creation of friendliness, compassion, pleasure and equanimity

(No. 2), self-discipline (*niyama*), i.e. purity and contentedness, is matched by (no. 2) the meditative creation of friendliness, compassion, pleasure and equanimity (a quartet known from Buddhism) in Part B. Thus, the imitator has followed Patañjali by also placing a moral conduct of living at the beginning of his eightfold path.

3) Sitting Posture (*āsana*) (§ P17-19) *sthira(-sukham) āsanam*	(3) exhaling or stretching of the breath,
(4) Breath Control (§ P20-24)	(4) contemplation of an object of sense (*viṣaya*) in a 'solid state of mind' (*manasaḥ sthiti*)

Both ways to deliverance continue in a similar way. They are not in exact accordance, but correspond nevertheless, in a way, as if the imitator would not have completely understood Patañjali's procedure to deliverance. For example, breath control in Part B is not prepared by a suitable sitting posture. But it is remarkable that the 'firm' (*sthira*) position of Part P finds its reproduction in the 'firm state (*sthiti*) of mind' in Part B.

(5) Drawing Back the Sense Organs (§ P25-26) 'Drawing back the sense organs is – as it were – the imitation of mere thoughts (of the objects) by the thinking. In doing so, the sense organs are not connected with the material sense objects.' (P25)	(5) contemplation of light (*jyotis*),
(6) Steadying the Thinking (§ P27)	(6) contemplation of a sense object (*viṣaya*) 'without passion' (*vīta-rāga*)

Drawing back the sense organs from the sense objects (no. 5 in Part P) has its parallel in the contemplation of a sense object 'without passion' (no. 6 in Part B).

(7) Meditation (*dhyāna*) (§ P28)	(7) Perception dependent from dream and deep sleep
(8) Concentration (*samādhi*) (§ P29=YS 3,3)	(8) 'Meditation' (*dhyāna*) on an optional subject
	Dispassion (§ B40)
	Unification (*samāpatti*) (§ B41=YS 1,41)

Clearly, the imitator had difficulties finding a parallel for no. 7, meditation (*dhyāna*), it being the second to last exercise in Part P. It remains incomprehensible why he declared dream and deep sleep to be exercises of meditation in his position on no. 7. Anyway, he lets 'meditation' (*dhyāna*) appear as the last constituent (no. 8) of his minor path.

Be this as it may, Patañjali's major eightfold path ends with a mental state called *samādhi* ('concentration'). This word consists of two prefixes: *sam-* and *-ā-*, and a derivation of the verbal root √*dhyai*, 'to meditate.'[18] The imitator thought it fit to call his final point of meditation, *samāpatti* ('unification'), consisting of the same prefixes *sam-ā-* and a derivation of the verbal root √*pad*, 'to reach.'[19] He even went so far as to insert, after Patañjali's example, the highly problematic particle *iva* (see p. 43) into the sūtra which marks the endpoint and final objective of the yogic way to deliverance. He modelled his § B41 after Patañjali's § P29 (in Part P, cf. p. 43).

18 J. Wackernagel/A. Debrunner: *Altindische Grammatik*, Bd. II, 2, Göttingen 1954, p. 300.

19 The canonical Buddhists use the term *samāpatti*, as well, with the meaning 'attainment.' It comprises eight states of meditation, scil. the four *dhyāna*, and four so-called 'realms of infinity' (T. W. Rhys Davids/W. Stede: *Pali-English Dictionary*, repr. New Delhi1975, s. v. *samāpatti*, p. 686).

To sum up, Part B offers nothing substantially new to contribute to Patañjali's initial guidelines in Part P. The 'minor' eightfold path of Part B is an unconvincing copy of the 'major' eightfold path in Part P, a makeshift conglomeration of erratic terms.

After enumerating the eight constituents of his 'clarifications,' the imitator continues with the ultimate aim of these exercises. It is the unification (*samāpatti*) of the soul, the unification of 'percipient, perceiving and the perceivable.'[20] The soul, here termed the 'percipient,' (*grahītṛ*) becomes one with itself, the perceivable (*grāhya*). As the practitioner, the yogī, is devoid of all thinking, and thereby of all matter, he becomes one with the soul, 'as in the case of a classy jewel in such a way that he, whose brain-movements have disappeared, adopts the hue of whom he is standing on (i.e. the percipient, the 'soul'). The yogī has become one with his soul, with himself, and thus perceives only himself. Even the process of perceiving (*grahaṇa*) has become one with its subject and object, with percipient (*grahītṛ*) and perceivable (*grāha*).

Swapping places of Part P and B

After the addition of Part B, one big question must be answered: Why today, in the text of the vulgate, does Part B have its place at the very beginning of the whole of the Yogasūtras, and Part P appears only after Part B?

The answer is easy. The imitator was so fascinated by his definition of yoga (§ B2), and so self-assured, that he simply put his second-hand Part B, which begins with just this definition, ('Yoga is the shutdown of the brain movements'), yet in front of Patañjali's original Part P. Since then, Part B, the imitator's addition, appears as the starting section of the handed down text. Patañjali's roots (Part P) and the imitator's simulation (Part B) have swapped places.

Moreover, the imitator must have had enough scholarly authority to impose his new version of the Yogasūtras on his pupils and finally on the mainstream tradition of yoga. He pushed the 'switched' new version through, albeit under the traditional name of 'Pātañjala'-yoga-sūtrāṇi.'

Thus, the earliest model, what I named *Yogasūtra, version 1.0.*, or Part P, was first increased, then distorted by Part B; and both Parts P and B together can be reconstructed as being Yogasūtra, the increased *version 2.0.* and the distorted version *2.1.*, consisting of the following paragraphs:

Yogasūtra, version 2.0. (before swapping places): § P1-16 (=YS 2,17-32); § P17-26 (=YS 2,46-55) P27-29 (=YS 3,1-3). § B1-11 (=YS 1,1-11); § B12-25 (=YS 2,3-16); § B29-39 (=YS 1,29-39); § B40-41 (=YS 1,15-16).

Yogasūtra, version 2.1. (after swapping places): § B1-11 (=YS 1,1-11); § B12-25 (=YS 2,3-16); § B29-39 (=YS 1,29-39); § B40-41 (=YS 1,15-16). § P1-16 (=YS 2,17-32); § P17-26 (=YS 2,46-55) P27-29 (=YS 3,1-3).

20 § B41 (=YS 1,41).

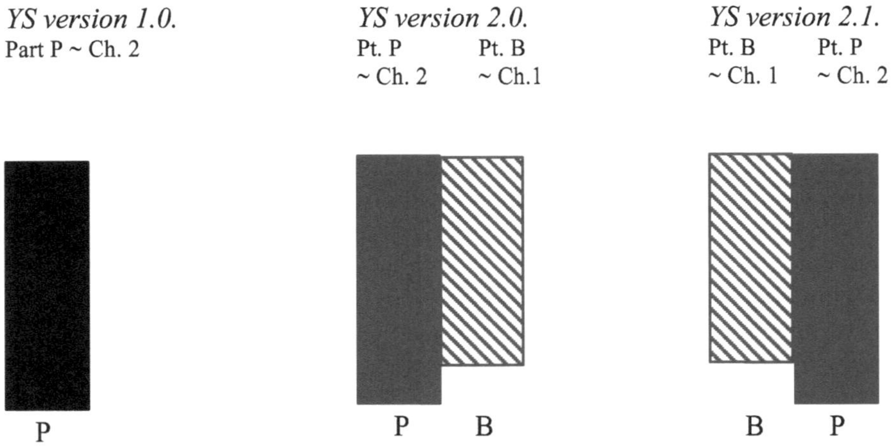

The Conjurer: Part C, the Siddhis

Patañjali's urtext of the Yogasūtras is characterised by *a strictly rational approach.* The 'non-existence of ignorance' shall produce the insight in the fundamental difference between matter and soul, an insight induced by the mental state of 'concentration' (*samādhi*). 'Concentration' is the endpoint of the eightfold path to deliverance.

All the more reason to be surprised to learn at the beginning of Part C,[1] that the last three steps of the eightfold path shall furthermore be combined, in order to form just another kind of exercise, called 'interconnection' (*saṃyama*).

Moreover, not only the state of 'concentration,' but also the 'shutdown of the brain movements'[2] and the exercise of 'one-pointedness'[3] shall be transformed. The new objective – after having reached redemption! – is to acquire the ability to perform 'supernatural faculties,' called *siddhi*, literally 'perfections.'

These perfections concern not only features like the recognition of one's own previous births or reading the minds of other people, but supernatural strength, like an elephant, or divine hearing. One of the widest known yoga wonders is the so-called

1 § C01-05 (=YS 3,4-8).

2 As described in § B41 (=YS 1,41).

3 The term 'one-pointedness' (*ekâgratā*) occurs in the YS only in § C3 and C4, the synonym *aikâgrya* is used once (in § E12). At none of these places an explanation is given. Both terms appear to be adopted from Buddhism, where they mean 'peace (of mind)' or 'unification (of cognizances)' (*Critical Pāli Dictionary*, s. v. *ekaggatā* and *ekagga*), which does not help to clarify the meaning. The Pāli derivations seem to be exchangeable with *samādhi*.

ākāśa-gamana, 'walking through the air,' or levitation. Of course, such crafts are quite the opposite of what is intended by Patañjali's eightfold path, which is directed towards finishing the cycle of rebirth, and not to achieve extraordinary advantages in the never-ending rat-race.

One anonymous scribe who read these passages, could not abstain from writing in the margin of his manuscript:

> 'These [siddhis] are unfortunate add-ons (*upasarga*) during 'concentration' (*samādhi*), [but] 'perfections' (*siddhi*) during activity.' (§ C30 =YS 3,38)

The next scribe incorporated this glosse (explanation) from the margin (where it was written in the manuscript) into the main text of the copy he was writing down.

In short: Part C on the siddhis cannot be the work of the same man who composed Part P, that is Patañjali, but is an interpolation by someone I would like to call 'the conjurer.'

Yogasūtra, version 3.0., consisted of the content of *version 2.1.*, enlarged by § C01-05 (=YS 3,4-8) and C1-47 (=YS 3,9-55). At that point in time, the Yogasūtras must have had the following content:

§ B1-11 (=YS 1,1-11); § B12-25 (=YS 2,3-16); § B29-39 (=YS 1,29-39); § B40-41 (=YS 1,15-16). § P1-16 (=YS 2,17-32); § P17-26 (=YS 2,46-55) P27-29 (=YS 3,1-3); § C01-05 (=YS 3,4-8) and C1-47 (=YS 3,9-55).

YS version 3.0.

YS version 4.0.

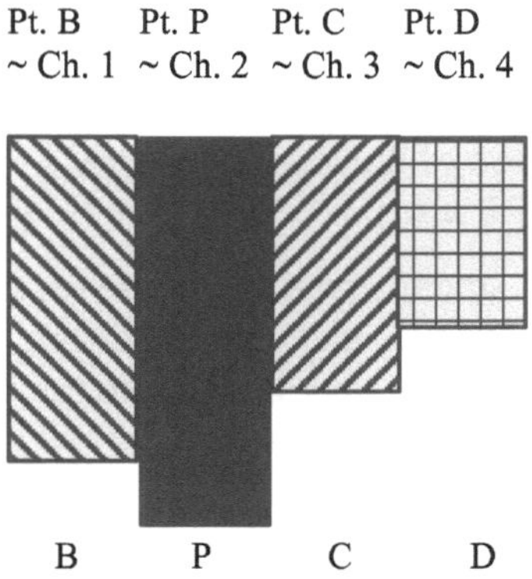

The Gatherer: Part D, the Miscellanies

The influences to the Yogasūtras that we have come across so far have been Patañjali and Buddhism, moreover the sections interpolated by the 'imitator' (Part B) and the 'conjurer' (Part C). Of course, there were more currents and trends that went under the name of yoga. These were not only various theoretical ideas, but also ready-made sūtras. Some unknown revisor and editor considered these materials so very indispensable that he did not dare to sort them out. I would like to call him 'the gatherer.'

He accumulated any odd passages, even if they were quite heterogeneous in their content, and incorporated them in the Yogasūtras of Patañjali. Now they form a kind of annexe, after the Part C on the supernatural faculties, which were already contradictory to what Patañjali had taught.

It is difficult to discover any connection to Part D with the contents of the previous sections. The reader is confronted with an assortment of 'thoughts of rebirth'; thoughts 'born by meditation'; with possibly Buddhist inspired, 'entity factors' (*dharmāḥ*) and their relevance for rebirth, together with musings on potential correlations between thought, object and soul. A spurious definition of 'isolation' (*kaivalya*, scil. 'the retrogression of the material qualities which are devoid of the object soul'[1] concludes this erratic conglomeration.

Part D thus contains idiosyncratic additions which I call 'miscellanies.' They show very little, if any, correspondences with the previous parts. Their mostly enigmatic content must remain the task of future research.

Yogasūtra, version 4.0., was composed of the content of *version 3.0.*, enlarged by § D1-33 (=YS 4,2-34):

§ B1-11 (=YS 1,1-11); § B12-25 (=YS 2,3-16); § B29-39 (=YS 1,29-39); § B40-41 (=YS 1,15-16). § P1-16 (=YS 2,17-32); § P17-26 (=YS 2,46-55) P27-29 (=YS 3,1-3); § C01-05 (=YS 3,4-8) and C1-47 (=YS 3,9-55) and § D1-33 (=YS 4,2-34).

Smaller Additions and Modifications

The Interpolation of the Yoga of Action

The *yoga of action* (*kriyā-yoga*) is introduced in the paragraphs § E2-3 (=YS 2,1-2), and was added to the wording of § P16. In the increased version, enlarged by the interpolation of the *yoga of action*, § P16 became § E1 (=YS 2,32).

This § E1 reads:

śauca-saṃtoṣa-tapaḥ-svâdhyāyêśvara-praṇidhānāni niyamāḥ.
'Purity and contentedness, (and also) penance, private studies
and devotion to the god are the moral precepts.'

The criticism of the content provides strong arguments that only purity (*śauca*) and contentedness had been part of the urtext of this sūtra (§ P16).

Penance, private studies and devotion to the god have only been added later. These three virtues diametrically contradict the spirit of Patañjali's teachings, which is, as we have seen above, deeply characterised by rationalism and intellectual independence:

- Penance belongs to the magical worldview.
- Private studies refer to the traditional scholarship of the Veda.
- Devotion to the god ignores the yogic endeavour for spiritual individuality.
- The three together constitute the *yoga of action*, as we are informed in the next paragraph, which reads:

1 § D33 (=YS 4,34).

tapaḥ-svâdhyāyeśvara-praṇidhānāni kriyā-yogaḥ.
Penance, private studies and devotion to the god
are the *yoga of action.* (§ E2=YS 2,1)

This *yoga of action* was considered to be so important by an unknown revisor that he felt compelled to add its content to the 'moral precepts' (*niyama*).

The moral precepts of Patañjali initially consisted of two virtues. The *yoga of action* is divided into three. As the no. 1 of the eightfold path (the moral prohibitions) counts five components, the interpolator of the *yoga of action* was encouraged to complete the two initial virtues (purity and contentedness) by three more assets in order to add up to the number five. Such games with numbers were quite popular with old Indian authors, if we compare, for example, titles of books such as *Pañcatantra* ('Having Five Chapters') or the Buddhist *Mahācattārīsaka-Sutta* ('The Great Sermon on the Forty,' scil. parts or constituents, cf. p. 36).

The text of the interpolation with the *yoga of action* continues:

samādhi-bhāvanârthaḥ kleśa-tanūkaraṇârthaś ca.
The *yoga of action* aims at the meditative creation of 'concentration' (*samādhi*)
and the thinning out of the 'defilements' (*kleśa*). (§ E3=YS 2,2)

Obviously, the § E2 and E3 were interpolated together, during one and the same redaction. Together, they transport the idea of the *yoga of action.* They were interpolated after § P16, because the fresh terms 'penance', 'private studies' and 'devotion to the god' (which had not yet been contained in Patañjali's wording) demanded an explanation.

To sum up: Patañjali's original wording of no. 2 of his eightfold path read:

'Purity and contentedness are the moral precepts.' (§ P16)

An advocate of the *yoga of action* added the three points: penance, private studies and devotion to the god. Enlarged by this interpolation, the sūtra now reads:

'Purity and contentedness, (and also) penance, private studies
and devotion to the god are the moral precepts.' (§ E1)

Because this interpolator felt the need to explain the enlarged content, he (or some of the following scribes) added the next two sūtras which sound quite like a *commentary* on and even a *justification* of the interpolation:

'Penance, private studies and devotion to the god are the yog*a of action.*'
(§ E2=YS 2,1)

And:

'(The *yoga of action*) aims at the meditative creation
of "concentration" (*samādhi*) and the
thinning out of the "defilements" (*kleśa*).' (§ E3=YS 2,2)

The Dislocation of the Yoga of Action

In the previous chapter I have given the reasons why the short passage dealing with the *yoga of action* must have been interpolated in the context of the major eightfold path of Patañjali's Part P. In the text of the vulgate, however, we find both sūtras (YS 2,1 = § E2 and YS 2,2 = § E3) on the *yoga of action* at a quite different place, devoid of any context, namely as the opening of the second 'chapter' of the vulgate. How can that possibly be explained?

We have to assume that the Yogasūtras were handed down predominantly not written on manuscripts, but orally: they were memorised meticulously. Some irregularities of the text can therefore be explained by the circumstances and compulsions of oral tradition. Like, for example, the seemingly rather arbitrary location of the two sūtras dealing with the *yoga of action*.

After the great swapping of Part B in front of Part P (see p. 15), the whole of the Yogasūtras commenced with a sūtra that belongs to Part B, namely a definition of yoga:

'Yoga is the shutdown of the brain movements.' (YS 1,2 = § B2)

The wording of the *yoga of action* is a very similar definition of yoga:

'Penance, private studies and devotion to the god
are the *yoga of action*.' (§ E2)

If you need a snappy introduction for a second chapter, nothing be more convenient than this second definition of yoga. And so it happened that the two closely connected maxims (§ E2-3) were taken out of their natural surroundings and now serve as the beginning sūtras of the second 'chapter' of the vulgate (YS 2,1-2). It must not be explained that in oral tradition, such a switch or dislocation could be more easily managed than under the conditions of copying manuscripts.

The Dislocation of the 'Defilements'

Another instance of the effects of oral tradition, which moreover is directly related to the switching of the *yoga of action*, is the dislocation of a whole passage of sūtras, namely those that deal with the 'defilements' (*kleśa*).[2]

In the text of the vulgate, we read, as early as in the fifth sūtra:

[There are] five kinds of [brain] movements,
[each] defiled and undefiled. (YS 1,5 = § B5)

As can be expected, the following sūtras YS 1,6-11 (= § B6-11) explicate, one after the other, the five kinds of brain movements. We would also expect, in analogy, that the defilements of the brain movements would be dealt with as well. But this is not the case. Instead, we find the explanation of the 'defilements' at a rather distant place, in the second 'chapter' of the vulgate, directly after the two sūtras containing the

2 § B12-25 (=YS 2,3-16).

yoga of action. So what is the reason for this irritating dislocation?

We recall that § E3 (which meanwhile serves as the second sūtra of 'chapter' 2 of the vulgate = YS 2,2) reads: '(The *yoga of action*) aims at the meditative creation of "concentration" and the thinning out of the *defilements*.'

Here we have found the explanation: The putting forward of this section in the text of the vulgate was caused by the occurrence of the 'defilements', of the term *kleśa*, in § E3 (=YS 2,2). This must have been the reason why some redactor thought it necessary to let the passage on the defilements follow only after YS 2,2 (= § E3), and not at its original place in the first 'chapter' of the vulgate, following YS 1,11 (= § B11). In oral tradition it was quite easy and natural, to switch the whole section on the 'defilements'[3] from their place in the context of the eightfold path to the new – and even more prominent – position after the *yoga of action*.

YS version 5.0.
Interpolation of the Yoga of Action

§ E1=YS 2,32 and § E2-3=YS 2,1-2

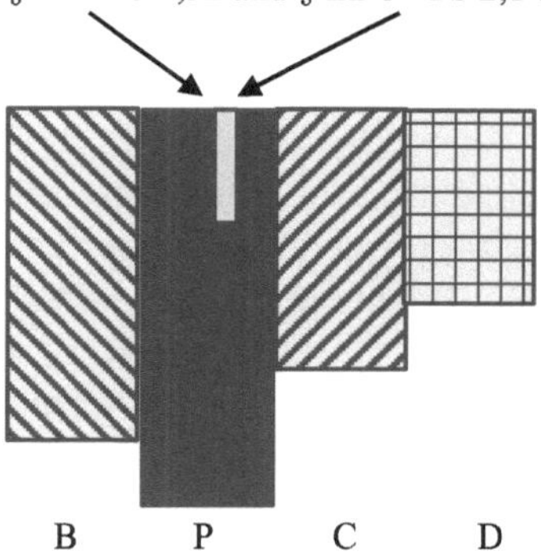

YS version 5.1.
Dislocation of the Yoga of Action

§ E2-3=YS 2,1-2

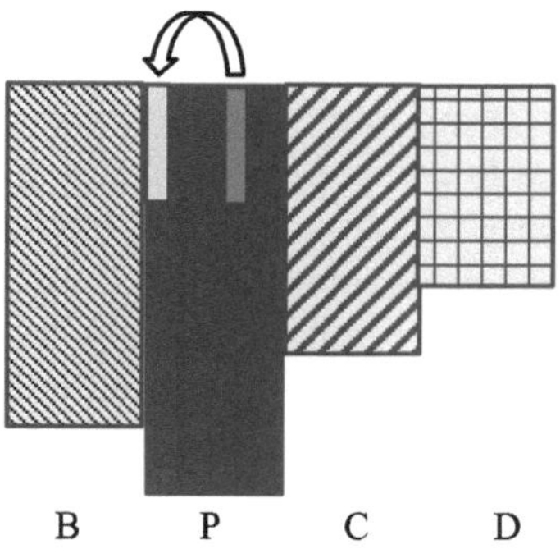

YS version 5.2.
Dislocation of the Defilements

§ B12-25=YS 2,3-16

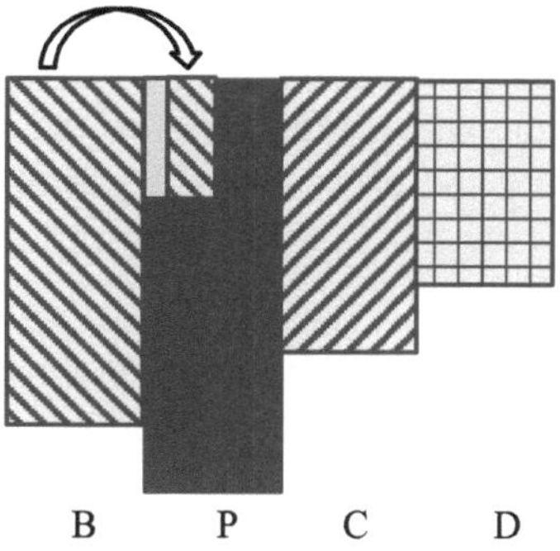

3 § B12-25 (=YS 2,3-16).

The Creation of the Opposite

§ E4-16 (= YS 2,33-45) deal with the 'creation of the opposite' (*pratipakṣa-bhāvana*). The passage is a kind of commentary on the first two components of Patañjali's eightfold path, i.e. on the moral prohibitions and on the moral precepts.

My scepticism regarding their authenticity can be substantiated as follows. The section contains several influences from various non-yogic movements and denominations, which one would be astonished to hear spoken by Patañjali. I do not mean the triad of greed, anger and delusion (*lobha-krodha-moha*), which are the arch-evils of Buddhism, because Patañjali, as we have seen, was not averse to Buddhist suggestions. Neither do I refer to a couple of rather banal and far-fetched remarks, for example the (admittedly quite entertaining) proverbial saying:

asteya-pratiṣṭhāyāṃ sarva-ratnôpasthānam.
On the basis of not stealing, all jewels approach. (E8)

Or the insight that 'chastity enhances potency' (E9). Of course it is a mere tautology to say that 'out of purity (*śauca*) should arise immaculateness (*śuddhi*).' (E12) Or, out of satisfaction comes an unsurpassable acquisition of happiness. (E13) All that is dubious, if not implausible.

But what is completely alien to Patañjali's sober intellectual background are references to the supernatural. For example, that 'not clinging to rebirth produces enlightenment concerning the circumstances of rebirth.' (E10) The proclamation that penance (*tapas*) results in 'perfection (*siddhi*) of the body and the sense organs' (E14) already sounds like the 'conjurer,' as I call him, who is responsible for the whole Part C of the Yogasūtras, dealing with the supernatural faculties, the siddhis.

The content of § E12 (= YS 2,41) is unoriginal, even tautological. There is a reference to the Vedānta philosophy of *ātman*. The whole paragraph § E12 is – to remove all doubts – formally marked as an admixture by the conjunction *ca* ('and,' 'and also').

References to devotional piety (*īśvara-praṇidhāna*, E16) and the recommendation to trust in a 'favourite deity' (*iṣṭa-devatā*, E15) in order to reach the 'perfection of concentration' (*samādhi-siddhi*, E16) prove beyond a doubt that the 'creation of the opposite' must be a spurious interpolation.

These doubts concerning the genuineness of the section on the 'creation of the opposite' are supported by the criticism of stylistic forms. The form of the 'non-philosophical comment' (see p. 4) is very rare in the whole of the Yogasūtras. An example would be:

Beauty, grace, strength and diamond-hardness
are the excellence of the body. (§ C39)

Remarks of this kind, however, occur in a cluster in the series of paragraphs § E9-14 (plus E6). This speaks strongly in favour of one unconventional interpolator, a maverick.

YS version 5.3.
The Creation of the Opposite

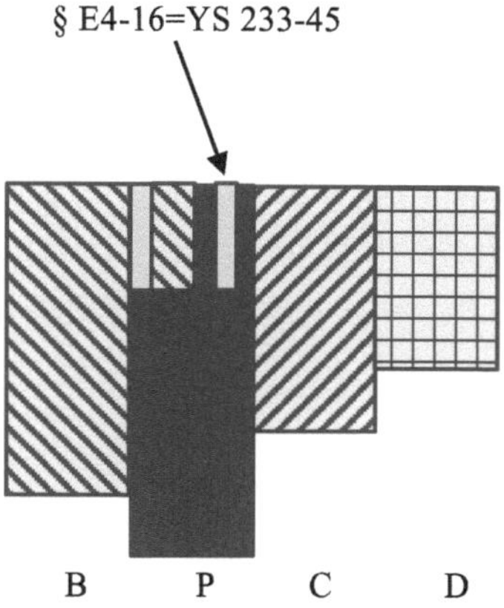

A Postscript to the Shutdown

The whole section § E17-22 (=YS 1,17-22) is a late postscript following the shutdown of the thinking. The passage must have been added by a revisor who felt that the text handed down to him was incomplete. He therefore wished to supplement it. § E17 reads:

> '[The shutdown of the movements of thinking] comes after calculating and reflection, bliss and egocentricity. Therefore it is conscious.'

Several inconsistencies must be pointed out here.

• (1) I fail to understand how the state of mind can be 'conscious' (*saṃprajñāta*), after the movements of the thinking have been shut down (*nirodha*).

• (2) The term *saṃprajñāta* ('conscious') is known from early Buddhist teachings. It has thoughtlessly been adopted from there. 'Calculating' and 'reflection' (*vitarka* and *vicāra*)[1] are also part of the Buddhist meditation formula describing *dhyāna*, which became one of the eight constituents of both eightfold paths of Yoga.[2]

• (3) 'Bliss' (*ānanda*) belongs to the monistic Vedānta system of philosophy. The term *ānanda* was borrowed from there and is incompatible with the dualism of Yoga and Sāṃkhya.

• (4) 'Egocentricity' (*asmitā*), being one of the 'defilements' (*kleśa*), has already been discussed and discarded previously in § B15.

• Moreover, the concept of 'insight' (*prajñā*), also praised in § E20, represents the Vedic worldview in § E37 (=YS 1,48), which has little to do with the concepts of yogic redemption.

1 *vitarka* and *vicāra*, also in § E31 (=YS 1,42) and B19 (=YS 2,33).

2 *dhyāna* being part of the 'minor' eightfold path of Part B in § B39 (=YS 1,39), and of the 'major' eightfold path in § P13 (=YS 2,29) and § P28 (=YS 3,2).

• 'Acute impetuousness' in § E21 possibly means the *longing* for deliverance. Of course, this is in contradiction to the 'dispassion' which is presupposed in § B26 (=YS 1,12) and § B40 (=YS 1,15).

• § E22 is to be understood as a commentary on the preceding paragraph. It eases the statement that 'acute impetuousness' brings the yogī closer to his deliverance.

YS version 5.4 and YS version 5.5.
Postscript to the Shutdown Devotion to the God

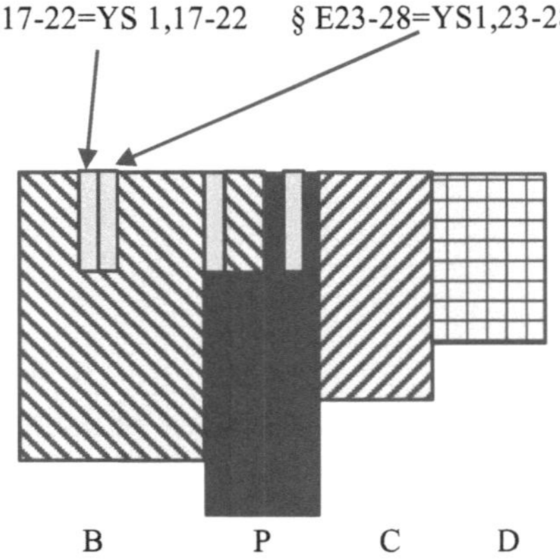

Devotion to the God

The subsequent passage § E23-28 (YS 1,23-1,28) has been added to Part B by an interpolator whom I would like to call the 'pietist.' His paragraphs deal with religious devotion to a favourite deity, recommending devotion to the god as a means to achieve the shutdown. It is therefore quite different in its intentions to the philosophical yogic path.

The term *īśvara-praṇidhāna* must be understood in the wider context of *bhakti*, 'devotion.'[3] As the Sāṃkhya system is moulded according to Viṣṇuism, the designation *īśvara*, 'god' or 'lord,' is likely to refer to the high god Viṣṇu, according to U. Schneider: „Sāṃkhya wird in ganz ähnlicher Form von den viṣṇuitischen Theologen vereinnahmt wie Vedānta von den śivaitischen."[4]

Observations on Tiny Irregularities

The following concluding two pages of the present chapter on *Smaller Additions and Modifications* list short observations (in the order of the paragraphs) on text-critical details. The cross-references are given in my notes after the

3 *bhakti* is also expressed in the paragraphs § E2-3 (=YS 2,1-2), E1 (=YS 2,32) or § E15 (=YS 2,44).

4 (Translation: 'Sāṃkhya is appropriated by the Viṣṇuite theologians in a similar way to how Vedānta is appropriated by the Śivaite.') *Einführung in den* Hinduismus, 1989, p. 116.

respective translations. These remarks are supposed to be consulted during the perusal of the pertinent sūtras. They are directed at readers who are especially interested in the textual criticism and are collected here in order not to unnecessarily tax the patience of the others.

§ C13-14 (=YS 3,21-22). The 'percipient,' the 'perceivable' and the 'perceiving' (*grahītṛ, grāhya, grahaṇa*) merge[5] in the final state of yoga meditation, the result of which is called 'unification' (*samāpatti*). Therefore, the 'potency' (*śakti*) or 'perceivable' (*grāhya*) category, which is explicitly mentioned in § C13, cannot belong to the category of matter, but is part of the soul. Nevertheless, § C13 encourages the practitioner of yoga to block this 'attribute' of the soul and, at the same time, disconnect himself from the sense of the other's sight in order to become invisible. The 'conjurer' (while drafting § C13-14=YS 3,21-22) apparently thought that the 'perceivable' (*grāhya*) belonged to the matter. Dealing with the *supernatural faculties*, he ignored the philosophical foundations of Part B, which is concerned with *spiritual redemption*.

§ C15 (=YS 3,23) see § E41.

§ C36 (= YS 3,44). There are many reasons to dismiss this sūtra as spurious.

• That eventually a movement (*vṛtti*, scil. *cittasya*) is still said to exist, is a clear contradiction to § B2 (=YS 1,2).

• The 'immaterialisation' (*videha*) of § E19 (=YS 1,19) is boosted here into a 'great immaterialisation' (*mahā-videhā*).

• *prakāśâvaraṇa-kṣaya*, lit. the 'disappearance of the veil over the [inward] light' occurred already in § P23 (=YS 2,52).

§ C42-44 (=YS 3,50-52) deal with the final stage of the spiritual endeavour of yoga, not in the religious perspective of the *unio mystica*, but consider it a supernatural faculty which results in powers like 'loftiness above all being and omniscience.' § C48 also belongs to this sequence of three sūtras § C42-44, because it uses the same terminology as § C42 by saying: 'When the soul is as pure as the benevolence (*sattva*), it is 'isolation' [of the soul].'

§ C48 (=YS 3,56) refers to § C42. § C42-44 (=YS 3,50-52) and § C48 (=YS 3,56) belong together; they are obviously of a spurious nature.

§ D24 (= YS 4,25) says that the erroneous identification of soul and thinking provokes the illusion of a 'self,' using the term *ātman*. *ātman*, however, belongs to the Vedānta philosophy and is incompatible with the Sāṃkhya/Yoga system. The paragraph thus presupposes the Vedānta tendencies and interpolations of § E36 (=YS 1,47), § B14 (=YS 2,5) and § E12 (=YS 2,41). Because it opposes it, this sūtra cannot be considered to belong to Patañjali's urtext, but is a very late, third-degree interpolation.

§ E29-30 (=YS 1,16-17) are third-degree comments on the imitator's definition of 'dispassion' (in § B40=YS 1,15). As to the philosophical term *puruṣa* for the 'soul'

5 § B41 (=YS 1,41).

(only in the post-Patañjali parts of the Yogasūtras), see notes on § B3; for the three qualities of the matter, § P2 (=YS 2,18).

Paragraphs § E31-33 (=YS 1,42-44) deal with kinds of 'unification' (*samāpatti*), which either are or are no more endowed with calculating (*vitarka*) and reflection (*vicāra*). This is an obvious contradiction to § B41 in which 'unification' has its place as the final state of meditation and is identical with redemption. In § E35 (=YS 1,46) this kind of unification is called *sabījaḥ samādhiḥ*, a 'concentration with seed.' So it also appears to belong to a heterogeneous, apocryphal line of tradition.

In § E36 (= YS 1,47) the influence of the rivalrous philosophical school of Vedānta, which calls the individual 'soul' *ātman*, is evident.

In § E37 (= YS 1,48) we find the influence of yet another spiritual tradition, namely of the magical Vedic world view. The *ṛta*, 'truth,' constituted the central concept of the Vedic speculation. It was deemed the original cause of all things, the main principle, 'das die Welt geschaffen hat und sie in ihrer Ordnung erhält.'[6] The Vedic Indians considered this *ṛta*, the 'truth,' as a 'magisch wirksame kosmische Potenz,'[7] which one can invoke and thus become able to conquer gods, spirits and men – the whole material world. In other words: by 'truth,' one can perform magic. Truth is magic-mighty.[8] Clearly, this kind of thinking is completely different from what we read in the sūtras belonging to the urtext.

§ E41 (= YS 4,1) is a late and apocryphal addition, because it deduces the supernatural faculties (*siddhi*) not from the triad of transformation (as in § C1-7), but ascribes them to 'birth, drugs, mantras' etc. It represents a heterogeneous tradition of yogic asceticism which stands a long way from the tradition which I call the 'conjurer.' The short addition that 'the recognition of death should result from bad omens' (in § C15) is very similar.

Having discussed the various tiny irregularities, we have also reconstructed and established the content of *Yogasūtra, version 5.0.-5.6.*

6 'that created the world and maintains its order' (H. Lüders: *Varuṇa*, 1951, 1959, p. 569).

7 'magically effective cosmic potency' (loc. cit., p. 405).

8 „Magisch-wirkmächtig". Cf. the author's article: *Wahrheit im Hinduismus*, 2005, pp. 35-53.

Yogasūtra, version 5.6

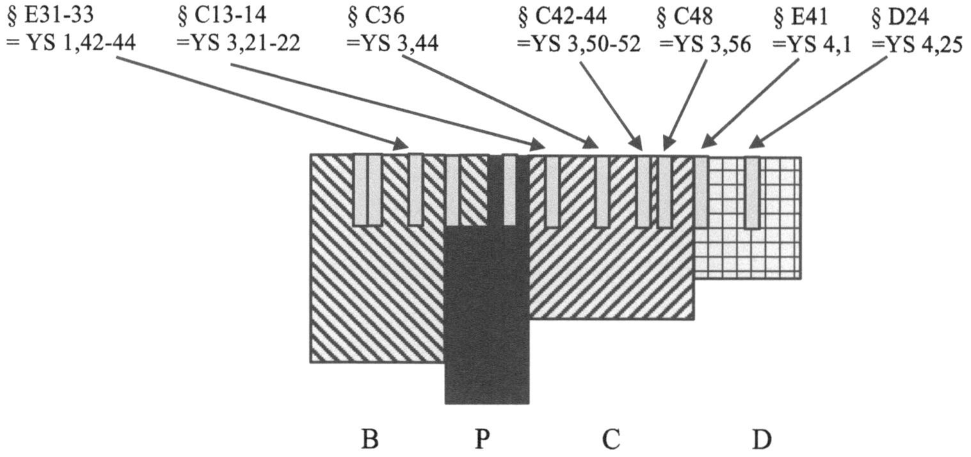

Yogasūtra, version 5.6. is, except for insignificant changes, identical with the vulgate. This is also the text with which the commentator Vyāsa was confronted.

The Curator: *Vyāsa and His Commentary*

Patañjali dates from the second century BC. After a tradition which lasted nearly seven centuries (a period of time that was continuously used for fresh interpolations in the text of the time-honoured Yogasūtras), a respectable scholar of yoga teachings wrote the first commentary on the treatise that is handed down to us. His name was Vyāsa, and he was not only a commentator, but also a responsible curator in the best sense. His commentary mirrors the knowledge of various yoga movements. The approach is encyclopaedic, not historic-critical. Vyāsa renders a most useful picture of the yoga teachings which were current in his time. But an uninterrupted succession from teacher to pupil, a *guru-śiṣya-paraṃparā*, between Patañjali and Vyāsa does not seem to have existed. Therefore Vyāsa's commentary does not reflect the inherent teachings of Patañjali's understanding, but the interpretations of the many generations of yoga adepts in between.

One example may suffice to illustrate Vyāsa's method of interpretation and its inherent problems. According to the classical system of the Sāṃkhya philosophy, the three qualities (*guṇa*) of the 'matter' are benevolence (*sattva*), passion (*rajas*) and darkness (*tamas*). Vyāsa refers to these categories when he explains (concerning the second paragraph of the Yogasūtras)[9] that brightness (*prakāśa*) is the nature of the quality benevolence, action (*kriyā*) that of passion, and firmness (*sthiti*) that of

9 § P2 (=YS 2,18).

darkness. Unfortunately, his explanation has the flaw that the Sāṃkhya terms *rajas* and *tamas* do not occur anywhere in the Yogasūtras.

This is a representative illustration of why the historic-critical analysis of the Yogasūtras must not be dependent on later commentaries (as is the method and habit of the majority of conventional yoga teachers), but keep itself restricted exclusively to the wording of the ancient scripture.

Within this methodical reserve, Vyāsa's commentary has remained, until today, the most important text witness of the vulgate of the Yogasūtras. Our commentator worked around 500 AD. The manuscripts and modern editions of the Yogasūtras have preserved Vyāsa's text with few insignificant variations.

Like Patañjali, Vyāsa also shows himself to be influenced by the rival religion of Buddhism. He adopted, for instance, the comparison of yoga with the four sections of the medicinal science:

> 'Comparable to the science of medicine that consists of four parts, pertaining to illness, cause of the illness, healing and medicine (i.e. diagnostics, pathology, therapeutics and pharmacy), in the same way our science (viz. the yoga) consists of four parts, namely: the cycle of reincarnation, the cause of reincarnation, deliverance and the means of deliverance – just so!'[10]

Here, Vyāsa, in his commentary on the Yogasūtras, speaks with self-assurance, for yoga – as compared with medicine – sees itself as the more comprehensive science. It is not concerned with the many little aches and pains (although the posterior Haṭha-yoga does offer relevant recipies). The original yoga aims at the destruction of the Great Illness – the universal suffering in the cycle of rebirths.

10 Cf. the author's: *Shivas Tanz. Der Hinduismus* ([1]1996) 2003, p. 71.

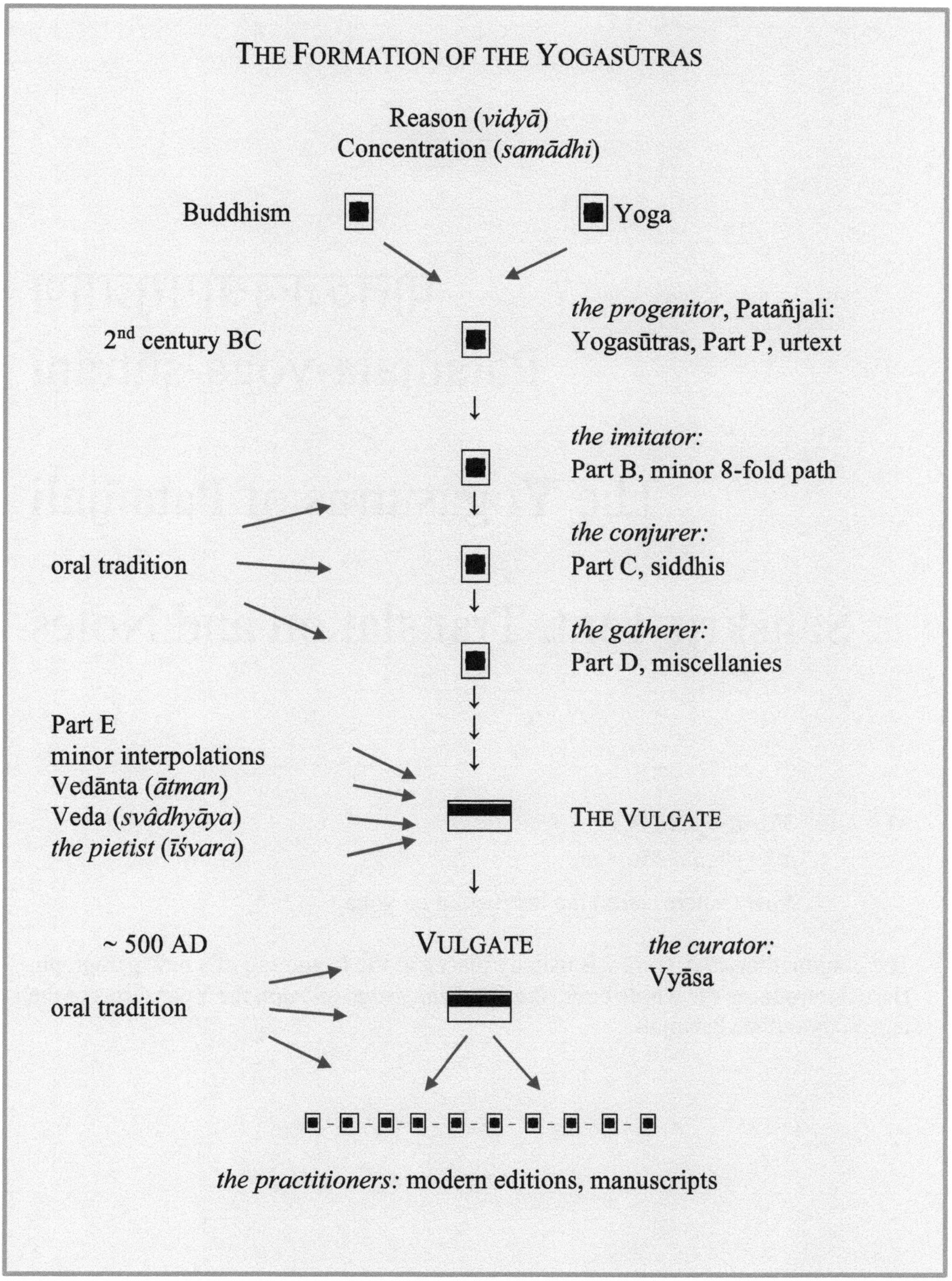
THE FORMATION OF THE YOGASŪTRAS
Reason (*vidyā*)
Concentration (*samādhi*)
Buddhism
Yoga
2nd century BC
the progenitor, Patañjali:
Yogasūtras, Part P, urtext
the imitator:
Part B, minor 8-fold path
oral tradition
the conjurer:
Part C, siddhis
the gatherer:
Part D, miscellanies
Part E
minor interpolations
Vedānta (*ātman*)
Veda (*svâdhyāya*)
the pietist (*īśvara*)
THE VULGATE
~ 500 AD
VULGATE
the curator:
Vyāsa
oral tradition
the practitioners: modern editions, manuscripts

पातञ्जलयोगसूत्राणि
Pātañjala-yoga-sūtrāṇi

The Yogasūtras of Patañjali

Sanskrit Text, Translation and Notes

YS 1,1 अथ योगानुशासनम् ।
atha yogânuśāsanam.

Now (= here starts) the instruction on yoga.

The conjunction *atha*, 'now,' is usually placed at the beginning of a new paragraph. Here it introduces the whole book, the *Pātañjala-yoga-sūtrāṇi*, the Yogasūtras of the legendary author Patañjali.

Part P

Isolation of the Soul
The Eightfold Path

§ P1-16 (=YS 2,17-32); § P17-26 (=YS 2,46-55); P27-29 (=YS 3,1-3)

§ P1-9 Theoretical Foundations
= YS 2,17-25

Abandon the Conjunction of Soul and Matter!

§ P1
= YS 2,17

द्रष्टृदृश्ययोः संयोगो हेयहेतुः ।
draṣṭṛ-dṛśyayoḥ saṃyogo heya-hetuḥ.

The conjunction of soul (*draṣṭṛ* , 'observer') and matter (*dṛśya,* 'observable') is the basic [obstacle] which must be abandoned.

Patañjali's Yogasūtras are addressed to those who are convinced that universal suffering is the main problem of human existence. In the cycle of reincarnation – so they believe – this agony is endless, and without beginning. The Yogasūtras teach a way for devotees who do not wish to be reborn over and over again.

Rājayoga, the royal yoga, is the intellectual yoga. It has only one purpose, and that is redemption. Right at the beginning, Patañjali names the central problem of human existence, the basic cause which must be abandoned: the conjunction of soul and matter. The fundamental error is the impression that the soul is a part of the matter. To abandon this misconception, – that is what yoga is all about.

Yoga is the *practical* side of the Sāṃkhya philosophy; nevertheless, in the beginning, the *philosophical* foundations must be named. That is why Patañjali starts with these theoretical preliminaries, encompassing the first nine sūtras. Very soon, however, immediately after this abstract preamble, he is going to concentrate on his true subject, the path to deliverance.[1]

1 § P14ff (= YS 2,30ff).

Having pointed out the main predicament, Patañjali continues by defining the attributes of the two categories of existence according to the dualistic Sāṃkhya/Yoga philosophy. First come the attributes of the matter, then of the soul:

§ P2-3 Attributes of the Matter
= YS 2,18-19

§ P2
= YS 2,18

प्रकाशक्रियास्थितिशीलं भूतेन्द्रियात्मकं भोगापवर्गार्थं दृश्यम् ।

prakāśa-kriyā-sthiti-śīlaṃ bhūtendriyâtmakaṃ bhogâpavargârthaṃ dṛśyam.

The nature of which is brightness, action and firmness, what completely consists of elements and organs of sense, which has as its objective, experience and avoidance, [that is] the matter.

The underlying philosophy of yoga is a dualistic world view that divides all existence in two metaphysical categories. Both are eternal and omnipresent.

• There is, on the one side, an infinite multitude of single *souls* that are conscious but inactive.

• And there is, on the other side, the one primeval *matter* that is unconscious but active.

According to the classical system of the Sāṃkhya philosopy, the three qualities (*guṇa*) of the 'matter' are benevolence (*sattva*), passion (*rajas*) and darkness (*tamas*). The commentator Vyāsa refers to these categories when he explains that brightness (*prakāśa*, here in paragraph P2) is the nature of the quality benevolence, action (*kriyā*) that of passion, and firmness (*sthiti*) that of darkness.

The activities of the five organs of sense (*indriya*, also highlighted in our maxim) are enumerated in the basic text: hearing (*śrāvaṇa*), sensing (*vedanā*), seeing (*ādarśa*), tasting (*āsvāda*) and smelling (*vārttā*).[2]

Avoidance, (*apavarga*) is the opposite of experience (*bhoga*).

§ P3
= YS 2,19

विशेषाविशेषलिङ्गमात्रालिङ्गानि गुणपर्वाणि ।

viśeṣâviśeṣa-liṅga-mātrâliṅgāni guṇa-parvāṇi.

Specific features and non-specific features, bare marks and non-marks [indicate] the divisions of the qualities [of the matter].

The question is, of which kind of matter are these 'specific' features (*viśeṣa*) of the qualities (*guṇa*)? The word *viśeṣa* can be found in the Yogasūtras elsewhere in two places, where it designates, on the one hand, 'special' features of the god Īśvara ('the

2 In § C29 (= YS 3,37).

Lord'), and on the other hand, of the magical 'truth' (*ṛta*) of the Vedic worldview.[3] These two can be taken as examples for the 'divisions' of the qualities of the matter which are pointed out here.

The 'marks' (*liṅga*) refer to subtle objects (as opposed to coarse ones). For, 'the realm of subtle objects finds its termination in the absence of marks.'[4]

§ P4 Attributes of the Soul
= YS 2,20

§ P4 द्रष्टा दृशिमात्रः शुद्धोऽपि प्रत्ययानुपश्यः ।
= YS 2,20 *draṣṭā dṛśi-mātraḥ śuddho 'pi pratyayânupaśyaḥ.*

The 'observer' (the soul) is pure 'observing.' [He may be] pure, yet he observes by way of concepts.

This is already a description of the *unio mystica* in the state of redemption. Patañjali describes the endpoint of the yogic endeavour as the identity of the soul (the 'observer,' *draṣṭṛ*), and its function or property ('observing,' *dṛśi*). During concentration (*samādhi*), which is the eighth and final member of the yogic way to deliverance, '...only the object is radiating and [...] it is – as it were – devoid of that which has the shape of the matter.'[5]

The soul does not 'observe,' as one would perhaps expect, the matter, but its 'object' is itself, and this is completely devoid of all matter. That is why it becomes one with its own function, namely 'observing.' There is nothing else to be observed.

§ P5-8 The Relation between Matter and Soul
= YS 2,21-24

§ P5 तदर्थ एव दृश्यस्यात्मा ।
= YS 2,21 *tad-artha eva dṛśyasyâtmā.*

To have him (viz. the 'observer,' *draṣṭṛ*, the soul) as its sole objective is the 'innermost nature' of the 'observable' (*dṛśya*, the matter).

Matter, however, behaves quite differently. Without its fundamental opposites, the souls, the existence of the matter would be pointless. Its 'innermost nature' is to observe not itself, or something that belongs to itself, but only its opposite, the soul, or rather: one of the innumerable souls.

This is the attitude of the dualistic Yoga/Sāṃkhya system, which was highly controversial already in ancient India. The Buddha, having overcome a monistic system,

3 The god Īśvara at § E24 (=YS 1,24), and the magical 'truth' (*ṛta*) § E38 (=YS 1,49).

4 § E34 (=YS 1,45).

5 § P29 (=YS 3,3).

metaphysical Vedānta (to be found in the Upaniṣad literature), retreated to an agnostic standpoint. He doubted that something like a soul (he called it not 'observer,' but *ātman*, 'self') could be found at all in anything of which a human being consists.

The Indian materialists,[6] based on a quite different, but also monistic standpoint, downright denied the metaphysical speculations of the Yoga system, and of any belief in the transmigration of souls whatsoever. *nâsti*, they said, *non est*, 'it is not.' At the exact moment of the death of a human being, the body completely disintegrates – they said – into the four elements: earth, water, fire and air, and nothing would be left. The body and the sense organs, according to their materialistic teachings, entirely consisted of these four elements, in addition to the objects of sense. The Indian materialists deemed the consciousness a function of the matter, it emanated in the same way as the power of intoxication from the yeast. Therefore with the disintegration of the elements, the consciousness, too, must disappear without residue. And because nothing will be left, there cannot be any afterlife or reincarnation. Therefore one should enjoy life as best as one can. Their hedonistic motto was:

ṛṇaṃ kṛtvā ghṛtaṃ pibet, yāvaj jīvaṃ sukhaṃ jīvet!
Go into debt, drink ghee, as long as you live, live in glee!

§ P6
= YS 2,22

कृतार्थं प्रति नष्टमप्यनष्टं तदन्यसाधारणत्वात् ।
kṛtârthaṃ prati naṣṭam apy anaṣṭaṃ tad-anya-sādhāraṇatvāt.

Although [the 'observable,' *dṛśya*, the matter] from the perspective of [the 'observer,' *draṣṭṛ*, the soul], when he has accomplished his aim, has vanished, it has not vanished, because it is common with that which is different from him.

The sūtra way of expression is an extremely condensed *nominal* style. When transformed into a more familiar *verbal* style, it reads like:

'When the soul has accomplished its aim (*kṛtârthaṃ*), when the 'observer' and the process of 'observing' have become identical and the soul finally observes only itself, because the conjunction with the matter has been abandoned, the soul does not take notice of the matter anymore.'

'Therefore the matter seems to have vanished (*naṣṭam*). But this appears so only from the perspective of (*prati*) the soul. For (*-tvāt*) everything else which is not a soul, has emanated from the primeval matter and is therefore different (*anya*) from 'it' (*tad*), that is: the soul.'

6 A materialist is called a Nâstika, 'denier,' or Lokâyata, 'worldling.' See E. Frauwallner: *Geschichte der indischen Philosophie*, vol. II, Salzburg 1956, p. 302ff. Suali, L.: *Matériaux pour servir à l'histoire du Matérialisme indien*, in: Muséon, N. S. [new series] 9 (1908), pp. 277-298. Tucci, G.: *Linee di una storia del Materialismo Indiano*. In: R. A. dei Lincei, Ser. 5, vol. 17 (1924), fasc. 7, pp. 242-310; Ser. 6, vol. 2 (1929), fasc. 10, pp. 667-713. Ballanfat, Marc: *Les matérialistes dans l'Inde ancienne* [partial translation of the *Sarvadarśanasaṃgraha*]. Paris 1997.

> 'But (*api*) just because everything else has emanated from the primeval matter, it has actually not vanished (*anaṣṭaṃ*) and is therefore common with it (*sādhāraṇa*), common with the matter, because it is also material.'

What is hammered in here, is the radical dualism of the Yoga philosophy, a dualism which endures even after the deliverance. It is the dualism of the countless, conscious, but inactive souls (the Lame One), and the one, unconscious, but active matter (the Blind who carries the Lame who – however – is able to see; *Sāṃkhyakārikā* 21b).

§ P7 स्वस्वामिशक्त्योः स्वरूपोपलब्धिहेतुः संयोगः ।
= YS 2,23 *sva-svāmi-śaktyoḥ sva-rūpôpalabdhi-hetuḥ saṃyogaḥ.*

The conjunction has its cause in [the false impression] that the two potencies 'matter' (*sva*) and 'soul' (*svāmin*) [both seem] to adopt that which has the shape (*rūpa*) of the 'matter' (*sva*).

- *sva*, 'what is his own,' is the 'observable,' the matter.
- *svāmin*, the 'lord,' is another term for the 'observer,' the soul.

Their apparent but unreal conjunction is based on ignorance:

§ P8 तस्य हेतुरविद्या ।
= YS 2,24 *tasya hetur avidyā.*

Its cause is ignorance.

'Its cause,' the cause of the erroneous assumption that soul and matter are combined.

Isolation (*kaivalya*)

§ P9 तदभावात्संयोगाभावो हानं तद् दृशेः कैवल्यम् ।
= YS 2,25 *tad-abhāvāt saṃyogâbhāvo hānaṃ tad dṛśeḥ kaivalyam.*

Through its (viz. of the ignorance) non-existence emerges the non-existence of the conjunction, that is: the abandoning. This is the isolation of the 'observing' (*dṛśi*).

The 'observer' is pure 'observing' (*draṣṭā dṛśi-mātraḥ*).[7] Here, we find the introductory definition of the state of deliverance, which will be reached by the last constituent of the eightfold path, scil. 'concentration' (*samādhi*).[8]

7 As we were taught in § P4 (=YS 2,20).

8 In § P29 (=YS 3,3).

The theoretical foundations for the state of deliverance have been defined by now. Patañjali continues by proclaiming the major eightfold path of yoga.[9]

§ P10-44 The Eightfold Path of Yoga (*aṣṭâṅga-yoga*)

= YS 2,26-3,3

§ P10-14 Reminders, and the Eight Constituents

= YS 2,26-29

The next three sūtras are to be understood as reminders for the practice of the eightfold path. They should be kept in mind during exercising. Before I present the three memory aids in detail, here is the gist of their content:

> Continuous perception of the difference is the means of abandoning the false impression of the identity of soul and matter. The insight in the difference will be attained by the last of the eight exercises of the eightfold path, called 'concentration' (*samādhi*). Concentration must be prepared and accompanied by seven preparatory exercises or 'members' (*aṅga*). Practicing these members will effect moral and spiritual purity. After the disappearance of the impurity by practicing the members of the eightfold path, the enlightenment of realisation sets in and leads to the perception of the difference between soul and matter.

§ P10
= YS 2,26

विवेकख्यातिरविप्लवा हानोपायः ।
viveka-khyātir aviplavā hānôpāyaḥ.

Continuous perception of the difference is the means of abandoning.

The 'difference' (*viveka*) is of course the radical separation of soul and matter.

§ P11
= YS 2,27

तस्य सप्तधा प्रान्तभूमिः प्रज्ञा ।
tasya saptadhā prânta-bhūmiḥ prajñā.

Its insight has bordering areas in sevenfold respect.

What is meant is the eightfold path. Insight arises from the constant perception of the difference between soul and matter. It is achieved by 'concentration' (*samādhi*), the endpoint of the major eightfold path of yoga, which Patañjali is now going to proclaim.

The Buddhist eightfold path also ends with 'concentration', and it is said at the beginning of the *Mahācattārīsakasutta* of the *Majjhimanikāya* and its parallel, the Chinese *Ārya-mārga-sūtra*, that it has seven 'members' (or divisions, Pāli *aṅga*). The Chinese parallel calls them seven 'branches' (支 *zhī*), being 'exercises, auxiliary

9 The 'major' eightfold path, § P10-44 (=YS 2,26-3,3), must be distinguished from the 'minor' eightfold path, § B32-39 (=YS 1,32-39), the last one consisting of the eight 'clarifications.'

disciplines and equipments.'[10] These early Buddhist parallels are quite similar to the 'bordering areas in sevenfold respect' mentioned here.

§ P12
= YS 2,28

योगाङ्गानुष्ठानादशुद्धिक्षये ज्ञानदीप्तिराविवेकख्यातेः ।

yogâṅgânuṣṭhānād aśuddhi-kṣaye jñāna-dīptir ā viveka-khyāteḥ.

After the disappearance of the impurity by practicing the 'members' (*aṅga*) of yoga, the enlightenment of realisation [sets in] and leads to the perception of the difference [between soul and matter].

The 'disappearance of the impurity' (*aśuddhi-kṣaya*) and 'purity' (*śauca*), which is part of the moral precepts (*niyama*) of the eightfold path, support each other.

At last the philosophical ground is prepared to start with the proclamation of the practical eightfold path of yoga:

§ P13
= YS 2,29

यमनियमासनप्राणायामप्रत्याहारधारणाध्यानसमाधयोऽष्टावङ्गानि ।

yama-niyamâsana-prāṇāyāma-pratyāhāra-dhāraṇā-dhyāna-samādha-yo 'ṣṭāv aṅgāni.

Morality (i.e. the moral prohibitions), self-discipline (the moral precepts), sitting posture, breath control, drawing back (the sense organs), steadying (the thinking), 'meditation' and 'concentration' are the eight 'members' (*aṅga*).

Patañjali now announces the eight members or constituents of the yoga path to enlightenment. U. Schneider[11] has shown that this yoga path was modelled on the example of the more ancient Buddhist eightfold path.

§ P14-15 (1) Morality (*yama*), the Moral Prohibitions

= YS 2,30-31

§ P14
= YS 2,30

अहिंसासत्यास्तेयब्रह्मचर्यापरिग्रहा यमाः ।

ahiṃsā-satyâsteya-brahmacaryâparigrahā yamāḥ.

Non-violence, truthfulness, not stealing, chastity and not clinging [must be observed according to] the moral prohibitions.

It is revealing to compare these yoga prohibitions with the first four rules of conduct of the Buddhist moral code (*śikṣāpada*):

• The Buddhist ban on the killing of living beings corresponds to the yogic 'non-violence' (*ahiṃsā*).

10 See the author's article *Sheng Tao King*, 1987, p. 235.

11 *Der Buddhismus*, 1997[4], pp. 84ff.

• The Buddhist 'taking of what has not been given' (*adattādāna*) corresponds to 'not stealing' (*asteya*).

• 'Chastity' (*brahmacarya*) is in literal agreement.

• And the prohibition of lying is in accordance with yogic 'truthfulness' (*satya*).

• Solely 'not clinging' (*aparigraha*) does not seem to have any correspondence with the Buddhist rules. Possibly 'not clinging' means something similar to 'zest for life' (*abhiniveśa*)[12], or, as the Buddhists call it, *upādāna*, 'seizing' or 'catching hold of,' namely of a recurring incarnation.

The most important rules of the Old Indian asceticism are summed up under this first constituent of the eightfold path, viz. (no. 1) morality. These rules are headed by the demand of non-violence (*ahiṃsā*). The taboo on killing initiates the yogic ethical co-dex. The first and highest duty of a yogī – and of a Hindu ascetic and 'holy man,' a sādhu, in general – is to avoid in thoughts, words and deeds every violation of any beings, human or animal.

Already in the middle of the third century BC, the emperor, Aśoka, the first Indian universal monarch, in his rock edict no. 1, announced the nationwide prohibition of slaughtering animals, be it on the sacrificial altar, be it in his own kitchen:

> 'No being must be killed here for sacrificial purposes. Formerly, in the king's kitchen, many lakhs of animals were killed daily for preparing curries. But now that this scripture on the dharma (the Buddhist law) is written, three animals only are being killed: two peacocks and an antelope, and the antelope not regularly. But neither will these three animals be killed in the future.'[13]

To the present day, India is dominated by vegetarianism, or rather lacto-vegetarianism: the Indians are great fanciers of all sorts of dairy products. Especially among the Hindu upper classes the consumption of meat is frowned upon.

§ P15 जातिदेशकालसमयानवच्छिन्नाः सार्वभौमा महाव्रतम् ।
= YS 2,31 *jāti-deśa-kāla-samayânavacchinnāḥ sārva-bhaumā mahāvratam.*

[Because these moral prohibitions are] independent of [the kind of] birth (or: caste), country, time and moment, [and because they] extend to all levels (*bhauma*), [the moral prohibitions constitute] a grand (or: serious) vow.

This conclusion plainly underlines the basic character of a moral conduct for the yogic deliverance.

12 § B12 (=YS 2,3) and § B18 (=YS 2,9).

13 See U. Schneider: *Die Großen Felsenedikte Aśokas,* 1978; U. Schneider: *Der Buddhismus. Eine Einführung*, 41997, p. 154.

§ P16 (2) Self-discipline (*niyama*)
~ YS 2,32

§ P16 ~ YS 2,32 शौचसंतोष[ौ ...] नियम[ौ] ।
śauca-saṃtoṣ[au ...] niyam[au].

Purity and contentedness [...] are the moral precepts.

§ P14 introduced the moral prohibitions (*yamāḥ*). Here follow positive counterparts, the moral precepts (*niyamāḥ*). The text of the vulgate adds 'penance, private studies and devotion to the god,' which is a late interpolation. Cf. § E1 and p. 18.

P17-19 (3) Sitting posture (*āsana*)
= YS 2,46-48

§ P17 = YS 2,46 स्थिरसुखमासनम् ।
sthira-sukham āsanam.

A firm and comfortable sitting posture [is required].

§ P18 = YS 2,47 प्रयत्नशैथिल्यानन्तसमापत्तिभ्याम् ।
prayatna-śaithilyânanta-samāpattibhyām.

By the combination of incessant endeavour and relaxation.

samāpattibhyām, in the dual, is translated here, in a practice-related context, by 'combination.' By the combination of incessant endeavour and relaxation, the sitting posture is both firm and comfortable. The endeavour is related to 'firm,' and the relaxation to 'comfortable.'

§ P19 = YS 2,48 ततो द्वन्द्वानभिघातः ।
tato dvandvânabhighātaḥ.

Thus there is no conflict of contradictions.

tataḥ, 'thus,' because of the combination of incessant endeavour and relaxation, it is no contradiction that the sitting posture should be both firm *and* comfortable.

§ P20-24 (4) Breath control (*prāṇāyāma*)
= YS 2,49-53

§ P20 = YS 2,49 तस्मिन्सति श्वासप्रश्वासयोर्गतिविच्छेदः प्राणायामः ।
tasmin sati śvāsa-praśvāsayor gati-vicchedaḥ prāṇâyāmaḥ.

When this is accomplished, breath control with adjournment of the succession of inhalation and exhalation.

tasmin sati, 'when this is accomplished,' i.e. when the sitting posture is firm and comfortable.

śvāsa-praśvāsa, inhalation and exhalation, heavy breathing, is one of the distractions (*vikṣepa*) of the thinking, which must be fought.[14] Exhaling or stretching of the breath is one[15] of the exercises called 'clarification of the thinking' in the minor eightfold path of Part B.

§ P21 = YS 2,50

बाह्याभ्यन्तरस्तम्भवृत्तिर्देशकालसंख्याभिः परि ।
bāhyâbhyantara-stambha-vṛttir deśa-kāla-saṃkhyābhiḥ paridṛṣṭo dīrgha-sūkṣmaḥ.

The movement [of breath goes] outwards or inwards, or the breath is held. It is kept in view regarding its location, time duration and frequency. [In this way it becomes] long and subtle.

The Bahuvrīhi compound *bāhyâbhyantara-stambha-vṛttir* is dependent from *prāṇâyāmaḥ* in § P20.

§ P22 = YS 2,51

बाह्याभ्यन्तरविषयाक्षेपी चतुर्थः ।
bāhyâbhyantara-viṣayâkṣepī caturthaḥ.

The fourth [kind of the movements of breath, in addition to those outwards, inwards and breath holding, effects that one] throws away the outward and inward sense objects.

The 'inward' (*abhyantara*) sense object could mean the impression of the 'outward' (*bāhya*) objects in the brain.

§ P23 = YS 2,52

ततः क्षीयते प्रकाशावरणम् ।
tataḥ kṣīyate prakāśâvaraṇam.

Then the veil over the [inward] light disappears.

prakāśâvaraṇa-kṣaya, lit. the 'disappearance of the veil over the light' also produces the supernatural faculty (*siddhi*) of the 'great immaterialisation' (*mahā-videhā*).[16]

§ P24 = YS 2,53

धारणासु च योग्यता मनसः ।
dhāraṇāsu ca yogyatā manasaḥ.

14 In § B31 (=YS 1,31).

15 Mentioned in § B34 (=YS 1,34).

16 In § C36 (=YS 3,44).

And the ability of the mind to [several kinds of] steadying (*dhāraṇā*) [is generated].

dhāraṇā, 'steadying' (the thinking) is the sixth constituent of the major eightfold path.[17] There, however, only one *dhāraṇā* is mentioned, so it remains unclear what the several kinds might be.

§ P25-26 (5) Drawing back the sense organs (*pratyāhāra*)
= YS 2,54-55

§ P25
= YS 2,54

स्वविषयासंप्रयोगे चित्तस्वरूपानुकार इवेन्द्रियाणां प्रत्याहारः ।
sva-viṣayâsaṃprayoge citta-sva-rūpânukāra ivêndriyāṇāṃ pratyāhāraḥ.

'Drawing back' the sense organs is – as it were – the imitation of [mere] thoughts (of the objects) by the thinking. In doing so [the sense organs] are not connected with the material sense objects.

The activities of the five organs of sense are: hearing (*śrāvaṇa*), sensing (*vedanā*), seeing (*ādarśa*), tasting (*āsvāda*) and smelling (*vārttā*).[18]

sva must be understood as a technical term for the 'matter,' as opposed to *svāmin*, the 'soul.'[19]

§ P26
= YS 2,55

ततः परमा वश्यतेन्द्रियाणाम् ।
tataḥ paramā vaśyatêndriyāṇām.

Out of this [arises] the highest control of the sense organs.

§ P27 (6) Steadying the thinking (*dhāraṇā*)
= YS 3,1

§ P27
= YS 3,1

देशबन्धश्चित्तस्य धारणा ।
deśa-bandhaś cittasya dhāraṇā.

Fixation of the thinking at one place is 'steadying.'

'Steadying' (*dhāraṇā*), meditation (*dhyāna*) and concentration (*samādhi*), the three concluding constituents of the major eightfold path of yoga, are brought here in close mutual connection.

17 Below in § P27 (=YS 3,1).

18 Enumerated in the late § C29 (= YS 3,37).

19 § P7 (= YS 2,23).

The genitive is post-positioned after the compound to which it refers.[20]

§ P28 (7) Meditation (*dhyāna*)

= YS 3,2

§ P28 तत्र प्रत्ययैकतानता ध्यानम् ।

= YS 3,2 *tatra pratyayâikatānatā dhyānam.*

What (during *dhāraṇā*) has only one thread of concept is meditation (*dhyāna*).

Meditation is an inter-religious phenomenon, a spiritual practice, which transgresses the denominations. It is a collective term that includes various psychological-psychosomatic techniques. The particular methods can be explained by differing religious contents. Patañjali, too, adopted the practice of meditation, which was not restricted to one certain variety of religious organisation, and combined it with specific yogic terms and concepts.

In the Yogasūtras we come across several terms and expressions which are used for certain techniques of meditation. Some of those are also known from Buddhist sources: besides *samādhi* ('concentration'), *smṛti* ('mindfulness'), *samāpatti* ('unification') or the four *brahmavihāra*, as the Buddhists call them (literally 'religious dwellings,' namely *maitrī*, *karuṇā*, *muditā* and *upekṣā*)[21] it is notably the word *dhyāna* that is used in the sense of 'meditation.' The Japanese word *zen*, for example in Zen Buddhism, derives from Sanskrit *dhyāna*.[22] As to Buddhist surroundings, *dhyāna* originally had no independent meaning. It was only adapted by the Buddhists, this adaptation being a concession to other, competing, religious sects, possibly to the doctrine of Ātman.[23]

dhyāna, 'meditation,' is attested already in the Elder Upaniṣads (e. g. Chāndogya-Upaniṣad 7.26 *ātmato dhyānam* or 7.6) or in the Bhagavad-Gītā (13.24)

dhyānenâtmani paśyanti ke cid ātmānam ātmanā
By way of 'meditation' some look inside themselves
at their self by means of their self,

20 As in § C3 (=YS 3,11) C4 and C31.

21 § B33 (=YS 1,33).

22 Imparted by Middle Indic *jhāna*. '*jhāna*' must have sounded very similar to *źi̯än* for Middle Chinese ears and was therefore (because the Chinese did not use a phonetic script) transcribed by a Chinese character 禪 with the pronounciation *źi̯än*.

23 For more details, see the author's article: *Meditation (dhyāna) in der ältesten buddhistischen Lehre*, 1990.

and is to be found later on in (most probably) all Indian religions. Patañjali defined it here in § P28 – very lucidly – as having 'only one thread of concept.'[24]

§ P29 (8) Concentration (*samādhi*)
= YS 3,3

§ P29
= YS 3,3

तदेवार्थमात्रनिर्भासं स्वरूपशून्यमिव समाधिः ।

tad evârtha-mātra-nirbhāsaṃ sva-rūpa-śūnyam iva samādhiḥ.

This exactly, when only the object is radiating and when it is – as it were – devoid of (that which has the shape of) the matter, is 'concentration' (*samādhi*).

Concentration (*samādhi*), the endpoint of the path to deliverance, the yogic version of the *unio mystica*, has already been discussed above.[25]

It must be added that the radical dualism of soul and matter is actually dissolved here. Dualism becomes monism. Patañjali has noticed this paradox, that is why he did not abstain from adding the particle *iva*, 'as it were.' This inconspicuous, tiny little word, however, transforms the whole sentence. What survives is just a metaphor. It means: the expected endpoint of meditation only seems like an *unio mystica*, it just appears like monism of the soul, – in reality the dualism of soul and matter continues.

Patañjali's imitator, the author of Part B, followed his leader's pattern meticulously, also in this respect. He also used the particle *iva* in the climax of his version of the yogic way to deliverance.[26]

artha-mātra-nirbhāsaṃ sva-rūpa-śūnyam are two Bahuvrīhi compounds dependent from *tad*, which relates to *dhyāna*, 'meditation' in the preceding paragraph.

24 The compound *eka-tāna-tā*, 'one-thread-ness' is an abstract of the noun *tāna*, 'thread.'

25 See the notes on § P4 (=YS 2,20).

26 In § B41 (= YS 1,41), see p. 39.

Part B

Unification of the Soul
The Shutdown of the Brain Movements

B1-11 (=YS 1,1-11); § B12-25 (=YS 2,3-16); § B26-28 (=YS 1,12-14);
§ B29-39 (=YS 1,29-39); § B40-41 (=YS 1,15-16)

§ B2-4 = YS 1,1-4 Yoga Is the Shutdown of the Brain Movements.

Part B is a second hand insertion by a redactor whom I call 'the imitator.'[1] He reworked Patañjali's Part P, trying to use a different terminology. Thus, he calls the endpoint of his path to deliverance not 'isolation' (*kaivalya*, like in Part P), but 'unification' (*samāpatti*). His 'unification' of the soul is to be achieved by the 'shutdown' (*nirodha*) of the brain movements. Therefore, his definition of yoga reads as follows:

§ B2 = YS 1,2 योगश्चित्तवृत्तिनिरोधः ।
yogaś citta-vṛtti-nirodhaḥ.

Yoga is the shutdown of the movements of the thinking.

'Movements of the thinking' is the literal translation for *citta-vṛtti*, the thoughts, or brain movements.

In order to separate the *soul* from the *matter*, it is crucial to realise that the thinking (*citta*) is part of the matter. The soul must not be misunderstood as a part of the thinking, but it is radically different from it. As long as the thinking is in motion, it masks the soul, because in that way the soul 'has the same shape as the movements of the thinking.'[2] Only when the thinking stands still, the soul can be recognised.

1 See the chapter on textual criticism, p. 9ff.

2 § B4 (= YS 1,4)

Therefore all activities of the thinking must come to a complete standstill, they must be shut down. Yoga is the technique to achieve this shutdown.[3]

§ B3 तदा द्रष्टुः स्वरूपेऽवस्थानम् ।
= YS 1,3 *tadā draṣṭuḥ sva-rūpe 'vasthānam.*

Then the soul (*draṣṭṛ*, lit. 'observer') stands apart from that which has the shape (*rūpa*) of the matter (*sva*).

The standard translation of this sūtra reads: 'Then the seer remains in his own shape.' This sounds easy to understand, and unsuspicious. But it is a wrong lay translation of a highly technical text that is overburdened with philosophical terms. To start with, *sva*.

(1) *sva*, in the usage of the Yogasūtras, is a term or appellation for 'matter.' *sva*, the 'matter,' is one of the two fundamental categories of being, or 'potencies' (*śakti*), called 'matter' (*sva*) and 'soul' (*svāmin*).[4]

sva has its secular or non-philosophical meaning 'own' in the Yogasūtras only in the phrase *svâṅga-jugupsā* ('aversion to one's own body') and in the term *svâdhyāya*, 'one's own or private studies.' The few places where it occurs in this profane usage,[5] are, without exception, late interpolations.

That *sva* cannot mean 'one's own' in the present paragraph, should already be clear by the opposition of 'matter' and 'soul.' A 'soul,' by definition, does not have a shape (*rūpa*) or form.[6] Matter, however, does.

(2) The substantive *sva*, 'matter,' is part of the compound *sva-rūpa*. This compound is, grammatically, not a Karmadhāraya ('the own-shape,' as in the false, profane translation), but a Bahuvrīhi. It means 'having the shape (*rūpa*) of the matter (*sva*).' The context of the preceding paragraph gives striking evidence that 'which has the shape of the matter' are the 'movements of the thinking' (*citta-vṛtti*), the thoughts, or brain movements.

(3) *draṣṭṛ*, the 'observer' or 'seer,' had already been Patañjali's philosophical term for the soul. I take this opportunity to list the terms for 'soul' as applied in the Yogasūtras:

- Patañjali employs the word *draṣṭṛ* twice in Part P. It is taken up by the 'imitator' from Patañjali here. The 'gatherer' will try it once.
- *svāmin* (the 'lord', the antithesis to *sva*) is also used by Patañjali.
- *grahītṛ*, the 'percipient,' is special for the 'imitator'.

3 The term *nirodha* for 'shutdown' is used only by the imitator, in § B2 and B26; once by the gatherer, in § C1; and in the interpolation § E40.

4 § P7 (= YS 2,23). *sva* definitely means 'matter' also in § P25 (=YS 2,54), § C28 (=YS 3,36) and § D21 (=YS 4,22).

5 *svâṅga* in § E11 (=YS 2,40); *svâdhyāya* in § E2 (=YS 2,1) and E15 (=YS 2,44).

6 The soul is pure 'observing.' (§ P4 = YS 2,20).

• *prabhu,* the 'lord,' is a late addition by the 'gatherer.'

• *puruṣa*, lit. the 'man,' is never used by Patañjali, but only by the 'conjurer,' the 'gatherer,' the 'pietist,' and by a late interpolator.[7]

(4) *ava-√sthā.* The basic meaning of *ava-√sthā* is 'to keep away from,' 'to keep clear of.'[8] *ava-√sthā* also means 'to stand (still), make a halt.'[9] Through shutting down the movements of the thinking, the soul stands still and has stopped fidgeting. Now the soul has become distinguishable and stands out from the matter. This brings an insight into the necessity (and possibility) of setting an end to the process of reincarnation, – and this is exactly what yoga is all about: redemption from rebirth.

(5) *tadā*, lit. 'then,' 'at that time.' Here I take *tadā* as having the meaning of *tadā prabhṛti*, 'from that time on,' i.e. from the moment in which all movements of the thinking have come to a halt.[10]

§ B4 वृत्तिसारूप्यमितरत्र ।
= YS 1,4
vṛtti-sārūpyam itaratra.

Otherwise [the 'observer,' the soul] has the same shape as the movements.

§ B3 and B4 are inspired by Patañjali's paragraph § P7 (=YS 2,23) which reads: 'The conjunction (of soul and matter) has its cause in [the false impression] that the two potencies 'matter' (*sva*) and 'soul' (*svāmin*) [both seem] to adopt that which has the shape (*rūpa*) of the 'matter' (*sva*).'

§ B5 Movements (*vṛtti*) and Defilements (*kleśa*)
= YS 1,5

§ B5 वृत्तयः पञ्चतय्यः क्लिष्टाक्लिष्टाः ।
= YS 1,5
vṛttayaḥ pañcatayyaḥ kliṣṭâkliṣṭāḥ.

[There are] five kinds of movements, [each] defiled and undefiled.

7 *draṣṭṛ* in § P1 (=YS 2,17), P4 (=YS 2,20), § B3 (=YS 1,3). § D22 (=YS 4,23). *svāmin* in § P7 (= YS 2,23). *grahītṛ* in § B41 (= YS 1,41). *prabhu* in § D17 (=YS 4,18). *puruṣa* in § C28 (=YS 3,36), § C42 (= YS 3,50), § C48 (=YS 3,56), § D17 (=YS 4,18), § D33 (=YS 4,34), § E24 (= YS 1,24), and in § E29 (= YS 1,16).

8 *ava-√sthā* „sich fernhalten", „sich entfernen" (pw). Apte too gives the meaning 'to stand apart, withdraw.'

9 According to Apte. The pw, s. v. *avasthita*, gives the meaning „feststehend, keinem Wandel unterworfen").

10 *tadā* occurs with the same meaning in three paragraphs of Part D, in § D15 (= YS 4,16), D25 (= YS 4,26) and § D30 (=YS 4,31).

The movements are the brain movements, lit. the 'movements of the thinking,' i.e. the thoughts.

§ B6-11 The Brain Movements (*vṛtti*)

= YS 1,6-11

§ B6
= YS 1,6

प्रमाणविपर्ययविकल्पनिद्रास्मृतयः ।
pramāṇa-viparyaya-vikalpa-nidrā-smṛtayaḥ.

[The brain movements are:] means of perception, error, imagination, deep sleep and mindfulness.

The five movements are explained in detail in the next paragraphs.

§ B7
= YS 1,7

प्रत्यक्षानुमानागमाः प्रमाणानि ।
pratyakṣânumānâgamāḥ pramāṇāni.

Evidence, deduction and tradition are the means of perception.

• (a) The word *pratyakṣa*, 'evidence' (that which is obvious or self-understood) occurs in the Yogasūtras only here.
• (b) 'Deduction' or inference (*anumāna*) refers to learning in general.[11] It is opposed to:
• (c) 'traditional learning' (*āgama*), or *śruta*, the *śruti* tradition, i.e. the Veda.

§ B8
= YS 1,8

विपर्ययो मिथ्याज्ञानमतद्रूपप्रतिष्ठम् ।
viparyayo mithyā-jñānam a-tad-rūpa-pratiṣṭham.

Error is wrong perception that is not based upon the shape of the object.

§ B9
= YS 1,9

शब्दज्ञानानुपाती वस्तुशून्यो विकल्पः ।
śabda-jñānânupātī vastu-śūnyo vikalpaḥ.

Imagination follows the perception of words and is devoid of objects.

The term *vikalpa*, 'imagination,' will occur only once more. There,[12] the author (or rather revisor) further elaborates that imagination is not only concerned with the formal aspects of 'the perception of *words*' but also with 'the perception of the *meaning* of words.'

The philosophy and also the mundane literature of classical India were keenly aware of the *difference*, but also of the *togetherness*, if not the *unity* of words and

11 According to § E38 (=YS 1,49).
12 In § E31 (=YS 1,42)

meaning, of rhetoric and hermeneutics. *vāg-arthau*, 'word' and 'sense,' are the first two words of Kālidāsa's epic poem, the 'Raghuvaṃśa,' the 'Dynasty of the Solar Kings' (early fifth century AD).

§ B10 = YS 1,10 अभावप्रत्ययालम्बना वृत्तिर्निद्रा ।
abhāva-pratyayâlambanā vṛttir nidrā.

Deep sleep is a movement which depends on concepts that are not (or: no longer) existing.

nidrā, 'deep sleep,' is to be understood as a twin of *svapna*, 'dream.' Both occur side by side in § B38 (=YS 1,38).

§ B11 = YS 1,11 अनुभूतविषयासंप्रमोषः स्मृतिः ।
anubhūta-viṣayâsaṃpramoṣaḥ smṛtiḥ.

If one does not let the objects be stolen which one has sensed, [this] is mindfulness.

asaṃpramoṣaḥ, 'non-theft' or 'not tolerating to have something stolen.'

Mindfulness (*smṛti*, in the Pāli *sati*), is of course a popular Buddhist term, as well as the meditational exercise, Pāli *satipaṭṭhāṇa*, which is grounded upon it. Since the promotion of the concept of 'mindfulness' by commercial Buddhism and the wellness industry, pertinent publications 'live as numerous as the stars' (to be seen in the Gobi desert).[13]

smṛti is – astonishingly – declared here to be an obstacle on the way to deliverance.[14]

§ B12-25 Defilements of the Thinking
= YS 2,3-16

§ B12 = YS 2,3 अविद्यास्मितारागद्वेषाभिनिवेशाः क्लेशाः ।
avidyâsmitā-rāga-dveṣâbhiniveśāḥ kleśāḥ.

(1) Ignorance, (2) egocentricity, (3) passion, (4) hate and (5) zest for life are the 'defilements.'

13 人民星居 *rén mín xīng jū*, to quote the Buddhist Chinese monk Fǎ xiǎn 法顯 desribing the people of Khotan 于闐, T 2085, vol. 51, 857b5-6. Fǎ xiǎn was a contemporary of Kālidāsa, both worked at the beginning of the fifth century AD.

14 It is praised however as a means to purify the mind of material thoughts (*sva-rūpa*) in § E32 (= YS 1,43).

§ B13-18 The Five Defilements (*kleśa*) in Detail
= YS 2,4-9

§ B13 अविद्या क्षेत्रमुत्तरेषां प्रसुप्ततनुविच्छिन्नोदाराणाम् ।
= YS 2,4 *avidyā kṣetram uttareṣāṃ prasupta-tanu-vicchinnôdārāṇām.*

(1) Ignorance is the [breeding] ground for the following ['defilements'], [be they] dreamt, thin, scattered or widespread.

Ignorance (*avidyā*) is the [breeding] 'ground,' lit. 'field' (*kṣetra*) for the following four defilements. Cf. § P8 (=YS 2,24) where it is said that ignorance (*avidyā*) is the cause of the erroneous conjunction of soul and matter. 'Lack of knowledge' (*a-vidyā*) is also the first constituent of the Buddhist 'law of conditioned arising' (*pratītya-samutpāda*), and stupidity is the main cause of suffering (not only) in the cycle of reincarnation.

§ B14 अनित्याशुचिदुःखानात्मसु नित्यशुचिसुखात्मख्यातिरविद्या ।
= YS 2,5 *anityâśuci-duḥkhânātmasu nitya-śuci-sukhâtma-khyātir avidyā.*

The perception of permanence, purity, happiness and the self (*ātman*) in impermanence, impurity, suffering and the non-self is (1) ignorance.

The content of this paragraph is exclusively Buddhist. It adopts the central concepts of Buddhism in order to give the yogic definition of ignorance. Ideas such as impermanence (Pāli *anicca*, 'impermanent'), suffering (*dukkha* – *adukkha*[15]), non-self (*anatta*) and, of course, ignorance (*avijjā*) are all taken from the very centre of the Buddha's teachings. Rich evidence can easily be found in the relevant entries of the *Critical Pāli Dictionary*, in M. Cone's *Dictionary of Pāli*, and also online in the *Pali-English Dictionary*, ed. by T. W. Rhys Davids and William Stede. To quote only one example from the Pāli *Dhammapada* 277 (and other places): 'All subconscious imprints are impermanent... all entity factors are painful, (they are) not the self.' (*sabbe saṃkhārā aniccā... dukkhā sabbe dhammā anattā.*)

§ B15 दृग्दर्शनशक्त्योरेकात्मतेवास्मिता ।
= YS 2,6 *dṛg-darśana-śaktyor ekâtmatêvâsmitā.*

The identification – as it were – of the two powers, 'seer' (*dṛś*, the 'ego') and 'seeing' (*darśana*) is (2) egocentricity (*asmitā*).

dṛś, the 'seer,' and *darśana*, 'seeing,' belong to the 'matter'. That is why they must not be confused with the soul, with *grahītṛ*, the 'percipient,' and *grahaṇa*, 'perceiv-

15 Pāli *adukkha* 'non-suffering,' synonym with Sanskrit *sukha*, 'happiness.'

ing,' which unify[16] at the endpoint of yoga, in the state of deliverance, when the 'movements of the thinking' (*citta-vṛtti*) will have been shut down.

Identification is not Unification.
Although the 'seer' and the process of 'seeing' (*dṛś* and *darśana*) cannot be compared with the 'percipient' and the process of 'perceiving' (*grahītṛ* and *grahaṇa*), because they belong to radically different categories of being, they *are*, as a matter of fact, compared here. That is done by the particle *iva*, meaning 'as it were.'

The 'seer' and the process of 'seeing' (*dṛś* and *darśana*) on the one hand, and the 'percipient' and the process of 'perceiving' (*grahītṛ* and *grahaṇa*) on the other, have a common property. It is the capacity to melt together (the seer with the seeing, and the percipient with the perceiving).

This melting together or blending is termed 'unification' (*samāpatti*) in the case of 'percipient' and the process of 'perceiving' (*grahītṛ* and *grahaṇa*). Both represent the part of the *soul*. But it is called 'identification' (*ekâtmatā*) here, in the case of 'seer' and the process of 'seeing' (*dṛś* and *darśana*), which represent the side of *the matter*.

Dṛś is not Draṣṭṛ.
dṛś, the 'seer', this must be emphasised, is therefore not (!) synonymous with *draṣṭṛ*, the 'observer' or 'seer,' as one might rashly think.[17] For *dṛś* belongs to the matter, whereas *draṣṭṛ* is a designation of the soul.

Dṛś is the 'Ego.'
dṛś, being a movement of the thinking, is roughly the equivalent of what modern psychology calls the 'ego.' When the 'ego' is not aware that it observes (*darśana*) itself, when the 'ego' and the process of observing have merged, this is our author's (the 'imitator's) definition of egocentricity (*asmi-tā*, literally 'I-am-ness').

§ B16 सुखानुशयी रागः ।
= YS 2,7
sukhânuśayī rāgaḥ.

(3) Passion is characterised by a karmic sediment of happiness.

§ B17 दुःखानुशयी द्वेषः ।
= YS 2,8
duḥkhânuśayī dveṣaḥ.

(4) Hate is characterised by a karmic sediment of suffering.

Passion and hate are a pair of antonyms which are explained in the previous and the present paragraph. Passion and hate are both relevant karma factors. To feel and act according to the emotions of passion and hate does not remain without consequences.

16 *samāpatti*, § B41 (=YS 1,41).

17 *draṣṭṛ* belongs to the same verbal root √*dṛś* as the nomen agentis *dṛś*.

Both effect a sediment in the subconsciousness. These sediments will be the cause of happiness or suffering, respectively, not only in the present life, but also in the next reincarnation. These karmic sediments are called *anuśaya*. The term only occurs in the Yogasūtras here (*anuśayin*, 'one who is characterised by *anuśaya*'). The term *anuśaya* is closely related to *āśaya* and *saṃskāra*.[18].

§ B18 स्वरसवाही विदुषापऽपि तथा रूढोऽभिनिवेशः ।
= YS 2,9 *sva-rasa-vāhī viduṣo 'pi tathā rūḍho 'bhiniveśaḥ.*

What is pregnant with 'matter' (*sva*) as its essence and what overpowers even an educated person, is (5) zest for life.

Apte gives a colourful description of 'zest for life' (*abhiniveśa*): 'a sort of ignorance causing fear of death; instinctive clinging to worldly life and bodily enjoyments and the fear that one might be cut off from all of them by death.' *aparigraha*, 'non-acceptance,' 'not clinging'[19] seems to be the antonym of *abhiniveśa*.

viduṣo 'pi... rūḍho: lit. 'what grows even for an educated one.'

§ B19-20 Getting Rid of the Defilements (*kleśa*)

YS 2,10-11

§ B19 ते प्रतिप्रसवहेयाः सूक्ष्माः ।
= YS 2,10 *te pratiprasava-heyāḥ sūkṣmāḥ.*

One can get get rid of them (viz. the 'defilements') by making them regress, if they are subtle.

§ B20 ध्यानहेयास्तद्वृत्तयः ।
= YS 2,11 *dhyāna-heyās tad-vṛttayaḥ.*

One can get rid of their movements by meditation.

If they are subtle, one can get rid of the 'defilements' by making them regress. If they exhibit 'movements' and thus are 'coarse,'[20] i.e. material, one needs meditation. The 'coarse' is – as opposed to the subtle – 'unfolded' (*vyakta*), i.e. visible.[21]

Meditation, *dhyāna*, has been defined in Part P, where it occurs as 'member' no. 7 of the (major) eightfold path of yoga.[22]

18 See § B21ff, and the *Glossary of Frequent Terms*, p. 105.

19 § E10 (=YS 2,39). As to *aparigraha*, see also my note on § P14 (=YS 2,30).

20 *sthūla*, § C37 (=YS 3,45).

21 According to § D12 (=YS 4,13).

22 In § P28 (=YS 3,2), see also § B20 (=YS 2,11); § P13 (=YS 2,29) and § D5 (=YS 4,6).

§ B21-25 The Root of the Defilements (*kleśa-mūla*)
YS 2,12-16

§ B21 क्लेशमूलः कर्माशयो दृष्टादृष्टजन्मवेदनीयः ।
= YS 2,12 *kleśa-mūlaḥ karmâśayo dṛṣṭâdṛṣṭa-janma-vedanīyaḥ.*

The root of the 'defilements' is a karma disposition (*āśaya*), of which one can make oneself aware of the current and the non-current rebirths.

The karma dispositions (*āśaya*) are the cause not only of the defilements, but also of rebirth in general. The term is similarly used in Buddhism too.[23]

It is stated by the 'pietist' that 'the god (*īśvara*, probably Viṣṇu) is [...] untouched by the karma dispositions (*āśaya*).'[24]

janma(n), 'birth,' is different from *jāti*, the 'kind of birth,' which occurs in the next sūtra.

§ B22 सति मूले तद्विपाको जात्यायुर्भोगः ।
= YS 2,13 *sati mūle tad-vipāko jāty-āyur-bhogaḥ.*

As long as there is a root, it (the karma disposition) will reach maturity, as a kind of birth, a span of life, and experience.

jāti, the 'kind of birth,' or 'quality of birth,' designates especially the caste affiliation. *janman* (also *janma*), in contrast, means 'birth,' 'rebirth,' 'existence.'

§ B23 ते ह्लादपरितापफलाः पुण्यापुण्यहेतुत्वात् ।
= YS 2,14 *te hlāda-paritāpa-phalāḥ puṇyâpuṇya-hetutvāt.*

Their fruits are joy and sorrow depending on whether they are based on merit or demerit.

The *fruits* stem from the the mature roots of the 'defilements.'[25] *puṇya,* 'merit,' is good karma.

§ B24 परिणामतापसंस्कारदुःखैर्गुणवृत्तिविरोधाच्च दुःखमेव सर्वं विवेकिनः ।
= YS 2,15 *pariṇāma-tāpa-saṃskāra-duḥkhair guṇa-vṛtti-virodhāc ca duḥkham eva sarvaṃ vivekinaḥ.*

23 Pāli *āsaya*, in the meaning 'dwelling place', 'basis', 'support', 'refuge', *Critical Pāli Dictionary.*

24 In the spurious § E24 (=YS 1,24).

25 Mentioned in § B21-22 (= YS 2,12-13).

On account of the suffering due to the [subconscious karma] 'imprints' of the torments of rebirth,[26] and because of the conflicting (*virodha*) movements of the [three] qualities of the 'matter,' all is only suffering for a discriminator.

The highly condensed *nominal* style of the sūtra will become easier to understand when transformed into a more familiar *verbal* style, like:

'Rebirth (*pariṇāma*) torments (*tāpa*). What causes the torment are the subconscious karma imprints (*saṃskāra*), which are responsible for the various kinds of suffering (*duḥkhair*). Another (*ca*) cause for suffering is that the three qualities (*guṇa*) of the matter (i.e. benevolence, passion and darkness) move (*vṛtti*) in opposite directions (*virodhāc*). Therefore (because of all these reasons), all (*sarvaṃ*) is only (*eva*) suffering (*duḥkham*) for one who is able to discriminate (*vivekinaḥ*) (these factors).'

'All is only suffering,' is an insight first expressed by the Buddha (cf. p. 102).

§ B25 = YS 2,16 हेयं दुःखमनागतम् ।
heyaṃ duḥkham anāgatam.

One must get rid of future suffering.

§ B26 = YS 1,12 Shutdown (*nirodha*) by Exercising and Dispassion

§ B26 = YS 1,12 अभ्यासवैराग्याभ्यां तन्निरोधः ।
abhyāsa-vairāgyābhyāṃ tan-nirodhaḥ.

By exercising and dispassion their (viz., the movements') shutdown [can be accomplished].

Having dealt with the brain movements and the harmful defilements connected with them, the 'imitator' begins a new section concerned with the exercises that should at last lead the yogī to redemption.

The shutdown (*nirodha*) mentioned in this sūtra refers of course to the phrase *citta-vṛtti-nirodha* at the beginning of Part B of the Yogasūtras.[27]

The terms 'exercising' and 'dispassion' can also be found as a pair together in a stanza from the *Bhagavad-Gītā* (6,35):

26 *pariṇāma* means rebirth here, as can be deducted from § D1 (=YS 4,2), where the 'transformation into [special kinds of] rebirth' is dealt with. It differs from the usage in the transition to the supernatural faculties (§ C01-05 =YS 3,4-8), where it should be translated in its basic meanng by 'transformation.'

27 *citta-vṛtti-nirodha* in § B2 (=YS 1,2).

asaṃśayaṃ mahābāho mano durnigrahaṃ calaṃ/
abhyāsena ca Kaunteya vairāgyeṇa ca gṛhyate//

(Speaker is Kṛṣṇa:)
Without doubt, o Powerful-One, the mind is hard to get under control, and it is fickle./ By exercising (*abhyāsa*) and dispassion (*vairāgya*) [however], o son of Kuntī, it is got under control.//

Most Hindus (not only the political fundamentalists) worship the 'Gītā' as their principal authoritative scripture. The *Song of the Exalted One* (so the literal translation of the name *Bhagavad-Gītā*) is part of the great Sanskrit epic, the *Mahābhārata*, and can be dated from the same era as Patañjali's Yogasūtras, scil. the 2nd century BC.

§ B27-28 Exercising (*abhyāsa*)
= YS 1,13-14

§ B27 तत्र स्थितौ यत्नोऽभ्यासः ।
= YS 1,13 *tatra sthitau yatno 'bhyāsaḥ.*

In doing so, the endeavour to stand still is 'exercising.'

tatra, 'there,' 'thereby,' 'in doing so,' viz. in trying to shut down the movements of the thinking.

§ B28 स तु दीर्घकालनैरन्तर्यसत्कारासेवितो दृढभूमिः ।
= YS 1,14 *sa tu dīrgha-kāla-nairantarya-satkārâsevito dṛḍha-bhūmiḥ.*

And if one has attended to it (viz. the exercising) for a long time without interruption and with care, one's [eight] steps [of the 'clarifications'] are firmly founded.

Here, the steps refer to the exercises called 'clarifications,' which will be proclaimed immediately.

satkāra does not only mean 'reverence,' 'respect,' but also 'care,' 'attention' (Apte).

dṛḍha-bhūmi: a Bahuvrīhi, 'one whose steps are firmly founded.'

§ B29-39 Distractions and Clarifications
= YS 1,29-39

There are barriers on the path to deliverance, certain 'distractions' which are responsible for the movements of the thinking. Concrete exercises, called clarifications, push back these distractions of thinking.

§ 29-31 Distractions
= YS 1,29-31

§ B29 ततः प्रत्यक्चेतनाधिगमोऽप्यन्तरायाभावश्च ।
= YS 1,29 *tataḥ pratyak-cetanâdhigamo 'py antarāyâbhāvaś ca.*

From there (viz. through 'exercising' and 'dispassion'), the mind also has barrier-free access to the interior soul.

pratyañc: The basic meanings of *pratyañc* are 'averted' and 'turning back.' It also means 'inner, interior; the individual soul' (Apte). The word *pratyañc* occurs in the Yogasūtras only here.

antarāyâbhāvaś ca, 'barrier-free,' lit. 'and [there is] the non-existence of barriers.'

§ B30 व्याधिस्त्यानसंशयप्रमादालस्याविरतिभ्रान्तिदर्शनालब्धभूमिकत्वानवस्थितत्वानि चित्तविक्षेपास्तेऽन्तरायाः ।
= YS 1,30 *vyādhi-styāna-saṃśaya-pramādâlasyâvirati-bhrāntidarśanâlabdhab-hūmikatvânavasthitatvāni citta-vikṣepās te 'ntarāyāḥ.*

Illness, rigour, doubt, carelessness, laziness, worldly attachment, mental confusion, failure (on the path to deliverance) and unsteadiness are the distractions of the thinking. These are the barriers.

avirati, 'das Hängen an den Sinnesobjekten' (pw); *virati*, 'indifference to worldly attachments' (Apte).

an-ava-sthita-tva, literally means 'unsteadiness'; 'Unstetigkeit, Unbeständigkeit; Unbestimmtheit' (pw).

citta-vikṣepāḥ, the 'distractions of thinking,' can, also in colloquial usage, lead to anxiety and even to vegetative reactions. In Bhavabhūti's play *Mālatī and Mādhava* (about 700 AD, ed. Kale, p. 13, l.8), for example, the Buddhist nun, Kāmandakī (who is normally of a quite even-tempered disposition), feels her left eye auspiciously throbbing (as if it were her right one) – caused by *citta-vikṣepa.*

The following sūtra elaborates:

§ B31 दुःखदौर्मनस्याङ्गमेजयत्वश्वासप्रश्वासा विक्षेपसहभुवः ।
= YS 1,31 *duḥkha-daurmanasyâṅgamejayatva-śvāsa-praśvāsā vikṣepa-sahabhu-vaḥ.*

Suffering, moroseness, tremor of the limbs and heavy breathing are the symptoms of the distractions.

'Inhalation and exhalation' (*śvāsa-praśvāsa*), i.e. heavy breathing distracts the yogī from the right path. The method to avoid this distraction is the 'stretching' (*vidhār-*

aṇa) of the breaths.[28] Again, the 'imitator' repeats Patañjali, who had recommended the 'adjournment of the succession of inhalation and exhalation.'[29]

§ B32-39 The Minor Eightfold Path, or: the Clarifications
= YS 1,32-39

§ B32 तत्प्रतिषेधार्थमेकतत्त्वाभ्यासः ।
= YS 1,32 *tat-pratiṣedhârtham eka-tattvâbhyāsaḥ.*

In order to push these (viz. the symptoms of the distraction of thinking)[30] back, [there is] the exercise (1) of [contemplation of] one [real] object.

Here begins a series of exercises (called the eight 'clarifications'), which is different from the 'eightfold path' in Part P, but also shows some similarities. The most striking one is – quite formally – that it also consists of eight constituents. In fact, the eight 'clarifications' appear to be modelled after the eightfold path of Part P (which again reminds one very much of the eightfold path of the Buddha). So, we can distinguish three different, but historically connected, eightfold paths:

- the eightfold path of Buddhism,
- the *major* eightfold path of the Yogasūtras, contained in Part P,[31] and
- the *minor* eightfold path of the Yogasūtras, contained in Part B, also called the eight 'clarifications.'[32]

The Buddhist eightfold path has influencd the *major* yogic eightfold path,[33] and this major yogic path has dominated the *minor* yogic path, which was modelled after it.

Both methods, the minor eight 'clarifications' of Part B, and the major eightfold path of Part P, are related, they can complement each other. The *minor* way, that of Part B, starts here, marked by '(1),' to be followed by '(2),' '(3)'... in the following paragraphs. The *major* eightfold path of Part P has been described above, in § P10-44.

tattva[34] means 'reality'; here it is an object which exists in reality (and is not just imagined). It must be distinguished from an 'object of sense,' called *viṣaya* (§ B37).

28 *vidhāraṇa*, § B34 (=YS 1,34).

29 In § P20 (=YS 2,49), as part of the 'breath control,' *prāṇâyāma*, § P20-24 (=YS 2,49-53).

30 *tad* marks the deixis of proximity and must therefore refer to *sahabhuvaḥ* in § B31, and not to *vikṣepa* (as the commentator Vyāsa thinks).

31 The major eightfold path, § P10-44 (=YS 2,26-3,3).

32 The minor eightfold path, § B32-39 (=YS 1,32-39).

33 U. Schneider (*Der Buddhismus*, 1997[4], pp. 84ff.) has shown that the yoga path is modelled after the more ancient Buddhist eightfold path.

34 *tattva* will occur again in § D13 (=YS 4,14).

§ B33 मैत्रीकरुणामुदितोपेक्षाणां सुखदुःखपुण्यापुण्यविषयानां भावनातश्चित्तप्रसादनम् ।
= YS 1,33 *maitrī-karuṇā-muditôpekṣāṇāṃ sukha-duḥkha-puṇyâpuṇya-viṣayāṇāṃ bhāvanātaś citta-prasādanam.*

By (2) 'meditative creation' (*bhāvanā*) of friendliness, compassion, pleasure and equanimity on objects associated with happiness, suffering, merit and non-merit, [arises] the 'clarification of the thinking.'

maitrī, *karuṇā*, *muditā* and *upekṣā* are four meditative exercises (called *brahma-vihāra*) of the Buddhists. Both yogic ways to delivery, explained in Part P and Part B, seem to be more or less influenced by Buddhist practices.

bhāvana (nt., not the feminine *bhāvanā* which we come across here, both with the same meaning) is a designation of two other techniques of meditation, viz. the muttering of the syllable *om*[35] and the 'meditative creation of the opposite' (*pratipakṣa-bhāvana*).[36] Both are interpolations.

§ B34 प्रच्छर्दनविधारणाभ्यां वा प्राणस्य ।
= YS 1,34 *pracchardana-vidhāraṇābhyāṃ vā prāṇasya.*

Or by (3) exhaling or stretching of the breath [arises the 'clarification of the thinking'].

There are, as already hinted at above, overlappings between the exercises of Part B and Part P of the Yogasūtras. The method of breathing taught here, being part of the *minor* eightfold path of Part B, is related to the 'breath control'[37] of the fourth constituent of the *major* eightfold path of Part P.

§ B35 विषयवती वा प्रवृत्तिरुत्पन्ना मनसः स्थितिनिबन्धिनी ।
= YS 1,35 *viṣayavatī vā pravṛttir utpannā manasaḥ sthiti-nibandhinī.*

Or (4) an activity (*pravṛtti*) has come about which is connected with an object of sense, [an activity] which [moreover] is marked by a solid state of mind [and thus arises the 'clarification of the thinking'].

The meaning of all this seems to be that the practitioner of this exercise shall meditate upon, for example, a random, but real, sound, or odour, etc., with the aim of clearing his mind of all other thoughts.

35 *om*, § E28 (=YS 1,28).

36 *pratipakṣa-bhāvana*, it is dealt with in § E4-16 (=YS 2,33-45).

37 *prāṇâyāma*, § P19-24 (=YS 2,48-53).

§ B36 विशोका वा ज्योतिष्मती ।
= YS 1,36 *viśokā vā jyotiṣmatī.*

Or (5) exemption from grief, connected with light [and thus arises the 'clarification of the thinking'].

In the paragraphs § B36-38 (=YS 1,36-38), the predicative noun *utpannā* (or *utpannam* respectively) ought to be added, meaning 'arises,' or 'has set in [during the exercise of meditation].'

§ B37 वीतरागविषयं वा चित्तम् ।
= YS 1,37 *vīta-rāga-viṣayaṃ vā cittam.*

Or (6) one thinks, without passion, about objects of sense [and thus arises the 'clarification of the thinking'].

The author of part B (the 'imitator') distinguishes between '[real] objects' called *tattva*,[38] and 'objects of sense' (*viṣaya*). The objects of sense are further divided in such to be contemplated 'in a solid state of mind' (no. 4, § B35), and 'without passion' (*vīta-rāga*).

§ B38 स्वप्ननिद्राज्ञानालम्बनं वा ।
= YS 1,38 *svapna-nidrā-jñānâlambanaṃ vā.*

Or (7) the perception is dependent from dream and deep sleep[39] [and thus arises the 'clarification of the thinking'].

§ B39 यथाभिमतध्यानाद्वा ।
= YS 1,39 *yathâbhimata-dhyānād vā.*

Or (8) by 'meditation' (*dhyāna*) on an optional subject [arises the 'clarification of the thinking'].

'Meditation' (*dhyāna*) has been mentioned above[40]; its definition is given by Patañjali in § P28 (=YS 3,2).

Here ends the exposition of the 'clarifications', which mark the minor eightfold path to deliverance, the method of Part B. It may consist of eight constituents, but is

38 In 'clarification' no. 1, § B32.

39 *nidrā*, already in § B6 (=YS 1,6) and § B10 (=YS 1,10).

40 In § P13 (=YS 2,29) and § B20 (=YS 2,11).

not explicitly described as having 'eight members',[41] like the major path of Part P, after which it is modelled.

§ B40 Dispassion (*vairāgya*)

= YS 1,15

§ B40 दृष्टानुश्रविकविषयवितृष्णस्य वशीकारसंज्ञा वैराग्यम् ।
= YS 1,15 *dṛṣṭânuśravika-viṣaya-vitṛṣṇasya vaśīkāra-saṃjñā vairāgyam.*

The self-restrained (*vaśīkāra*) state of consciousness (*saṃjñā*) of he who is not thirsty after objects he has seen or heard, is dispassion.

vitṛṣṇa reminds one very much of the role which *tṛṣṇā*, the 'thirst,' plays in Buddhism. Being a symbol for greed, the 'thirst' is the most prominent reason for all-encompassing suffering, according to the second of the Buddhist 'four noble truths.'[42]

§ B41 Unification (*samāpatti*) as the Aim of Yoga

= YS 1,41

§ B41 क्षीणवृत्तेरभिजातस्येव मणेर्ग्रहीतृग्रहणग्राह्येषु तत्स्थतदञ्जनता समापत्तिः ।
= YS 1,41 *kṣīṇa-vṛtter abhijātasyêva maṇer grahītṛ-grahaṇa-grāhyeṣu tat-stha-tad-añjanatā samāpattiḥ.*

To him whose movements [of thinking] have [waned and] disappeared, [occurs] a 'unification' (*samāpatti*) of percipient, perceiving and the perceivable, as in the case of a classy jewel in such a way that he [whose movements have vanished] adopts the hue of that on which he stands (i.e. the percipient, the 'soul').

The individual soul is only called *grahītṛ*, the 'percipient,' here.[43]

What is described in this maxim, constituting the climax and finish of Part B, is the aim of yoga, the point when the movements of the thinking are shut down[44] or have disappeared (*kṣīṇa*) and the soul stands firmly apart in the middle of the matter, with and for which so far it had falsely been identified or mistaken. Now, however, subject and object coincide, the 'percipient' (*grahītṛ*), the soul, becomes one with itself, the 'perceivable' (*grāhya*). It perceives itself and thus also becomes the process of 'perceiving' (*grahaṇa*).

41 *aṣṭāv aṅgāni*, § P13 (=YS 2,29).

42 See U. Schneider: *Der Buddhismus. Eine Einführung*, ⁴1997, p. 73.

43 See note on § B3 (p. 45) where I have listed the terms for 'soul' as applied in the Yogasūtras.

44 § B2 (=YS 1,2).

This state of the *unio mystica* is termed, in Part B, 'unification' (*samāpatti*). The 'meeting' or 'encounter' (this is the everyday, the non-philosophical meaning of *samāpatti*) of percipient, perceiving and the perceivable is to be understood in this sense of 'unity' or 'unification.'[45]

'He whose movements of thinking are waned and have disappeared'[46] is a description of the yogī who has meditated successfully. He adopts, as it were, the hue of the object on which he stands (i.e. the percipient, the soul). The yogī is standing apart from the matter because his brain movements have ceased to exist. In this way he is able to become one with his soul.

The identification of, on the one hand, the soul as percipient and perceivable, and, on the other, of the yogī and his soul, is expressed by the metaphor of the 'classy jewel' (*abhijāta maṇi*). The jewel adopts the hue of the object on which it rests.

samāpatti, the 'unification,' is synonymous with *samādhi*, 'concentration,' the endpoint of the major eightfold path of yoga in Part P, and also with *kaivalya*, the 'isolation' of the soul, as it is called at the conclusion of the theoretical foundations of Part P.[47] Thereby the aim of yoga is defined and the endpoint is reached.

An Excursus into Metaphorology

The image of the 'classy jewel' (*abhijāta maṇi*) can be analysed by the method and terms of ancient Indian poetology, the Alaṃkāra-śāstra, but also, with the same results, by modern Western metaphorology.

Both methods discern, firstly, a subject of the metaphor, the receiver of the image, or, in the Sanskrit, the *upameya*. This is the yogī (the *kṣīṇavṛtti*). Secondly the object of the metaphor, the provider of the image, or the *upamāna*, is the jewel. The jewel (*maṇi*) rests upon its base (*tat-stha*), the hue (*añjanatā*) of which it adopts. The yogī stands upon his soul and adopts its hue, which is a poetic expression for becoming one with it. This is the *tertium comparationis*, the common property or *sādhāraṇa-dharma*. The fourth element of a complete comparison (*upamā*) is the particle of comparison, *dyotaka*. Here it is *iva*.

This, however, is only one half of the image. The sūtra speaks of a 'unification' of percipient, perceiving and perceivable. It means that the soul perceives itself, in the same way as the yogī perceives himself, because he has become identical with his soul. Now the receiver and the provider of the image fall together in one and become identical with their common property: the hue of the jewel or the self-recognition of the soul = the yogī, respectively. I call this, when the subject and the object of a metaphor fall together into themselves, the 'implosion' of the angle of imagery.

The two halves of this metaphor have different 'angles' of the image. As to the first half of the metaphor, there is the angle between the human yogī and the

45 As to the use of the particle *iva* in both sūtras, see the notes on § P29 above (p. 17).

46 *kṣīṇa-vṛtti*, a Bahuvrīhi compound.

47 In § P9 (=YS 2,25).

inanimate element, the jewel. Concerning the other half, there is no angle of the image at all. The jewel is compared with itself, and the soul = the yogī with it/himself. This is, what H. Weinrich calls a 'bold' metaphor.[48] M. Jackmuth, in her analysis of Kālidāsa's imagery,[49] speaks of 'oscillation' of a metaphor, when there are different angles of imagery in one multi-level metaphor. Consequently, we can observe a similar perfection of imagery in the Yogasūtra as in Kālidāsa's masterful poems.

48 *Semantik der kühnen Metapher*, 1963.

49 *Die Bildersprache Kālidāsas*, 2002.

Part C

The Supernatural Faculties

§ C01-05 (=YS 3,4-8); C1-47 (=YS 3,9-55)

Part C is the work of a revisor and editor who relied on the work of his predecessors, Patañjali (Part A) and the 'imitator' (Part B). I would like to call him the 'conjurer.' He contributed those features which have moulded the popular appearance of yoga most: the miraculous crafts and supernatural faculties.[1]

Serious teachers like, for example, the Buddha, have disclaimed the performance of such skills, to avoid becoming associated with questionable practices of magic. The Buddha says (in a historically sound and therefore believable passage of the Pāli Kevaddhasutta) that such shows had been introduced by outlandish barbarians in India, as for instance the Greek. That is why they were known after the region of Gandhāra (today Afghanistan) in the north-west of India as *Gāndhārī-vidyā*, 'knowledge belonging to Gandhāra.' And therefore – continues the Buddha (showing unusual feelings) – 'I detest the miracle of witchery, I am ashamed of it and I abhor it.'[2]

It is not the duty of the historian of religions to judge the possibility or impossibility of such miraculous exploits. The problem of the facticity of the extrasensory is subject to the parapsychology. The historian of religions, in contrast, is not concerned with the miracle, but with the *belief in* miracles. He can state that in Hinduism, the belief in the possibility of such supernatural performances exists. It occurs not only in the Yogasūtras, but also in numerous other authoritative scriptures of the Hindus. Indeed, the comparison with other religions, for example, Christianity, shows that Hinduism stands by no means alone. The inherent desire of naïve piety for supernatural authentication has led to claims of miracles in presumably all religions.

Religion is the pursuit of otherworldly salvation: this is my definition of religion. Religious quests can result in the blurring of the borderlines between the sacred and the profane. In that case, all too easily, the phantasmagoria of the other worlds appear manifest in the here and now.

1 In the meantime, yoga seems to be typically associated with unconventional medicinal and wellness practices. Haṭhayoga, the 'coarse' yoga, has ousted the 'royal,' the Rājayoga.

2 See the author's: *On the Precanonical Shape of the Kevaddha-sutta as Compared with the Kien-ku-king*, 1993, pp. 67ff. – *A Translation of the Chinese Kevaddhasutta*, 1995, pp. 189ff. – *Buddhismus und Wunderglaube*, 1993, p. 77.

§ C01-05 The Transition to the Supernatural Faculties: Interconnection (*saṃyama*)

(= YS 3,4-8)

§ C01
= YS 3,4

त्रयमेकत्र संयमः ।

trayam ekatra saṃyamaḥ.

As a triad together (consisting of *dhāraṇā*, *dhyāna* and *samādhi*) [they form the meditation technique of] 'interconnection' (*saṃyama*).

The reference here is to the last three constituents of Patañjali's eightfold path, namely 'steadying (the thinking),' 'meditation' and 'concentration' (*dhāraṇā*, *dhyāna* and *samādhi*). These last three steps in combination shall form a new kind of exercise, called 'interconnection' (*saṃyama*). The exercise of 'interconnection' will be needed to accomplish the supernatural faculties.[3] (For the textual criticism on this and the following sūtras, see p. 16).

§ C02
= YS 3,5

तज्जयात्प्रज्ञालोकः ।

taj-jayāt prajñâlokaḥ.

By conquering it, the 'light of insight' [flashes up].

'By conquering it,' viz. by mastering the meditation technique of 'interconnection' (*saṃyama*) of *dhāraṇā*, *dhyāna* and *samādhi*.

§ C03
= YS 3,6

तस्य भूमिषु विनियोगः ।

tasya bhūmiṣu viniyogaḥ.

Its exertion in steps.

'Its exertion' means the exertion of the meditation technique of 'interconnection' (*saṃyama*) of *dhāraṇā*, *dhyāna* and *samādhi*.

The 'steps' (*bhūmi*) are the first seven constituents or 'members' (*aṅga*) of the eightfold path of yoga.[4] They are preliminary exercises or auxiliary disciplines, the 'bordering steps' of the last one, 'concentration' (*samādhi*).[5]

3 According to § C8ff (=YS 3,16).

4 According to § P11 (=YS 2,27).

5 See § B28 (=YS 1,14, *dṛḍha-bhūmi*), § B36 (=YS 1,30, light, *jyotis*), § P11 (=YS 2,27, *prânta-bhūmi*), and § P15 (=YS 2,31, *bhauma*).

§ C04
= YS 3,7

त्रयमन्तरङ्गं पूर्वेभ्यः ।

trayam antar-aṅgaṃ pūrvebhyaḥ.

The triad belongs to the preceding [constituents of the eightfold path].

The 'triad' is again that of § C01 (*dhāraṇā*, *dhyāna* and *samādhi*). The 'preceding' are the preceding five constituents of the eightfold path of yoga (no. 1-5), namely morality (the moral prohibitions), self-discipline (the moral precepts), sitting posture, breath control and drawing back the sense organs. The sūtra means to say that the eight constituents of the yoga path should be practised not one after the other, but complementing each other.

§ C05
= YS 3,8

तदपि बहिरङ्गं निर्बीस्य ।

tad api bahir-aṅgaṃ nirbījasya.

But it does not belong to the 'seedless' [*samādhi*].

'It' (*tad*) still means the triad mentioned in § C01 and § C04 *dhāraṇā*, *dhyāna* and *samādhi*.

bahir-aṅgam, 'does not belong to,' lit. 'is an exterior member.'

nirbīja, the 'seedless' means the 'seedless' *samādhi*, which is supposed to set in when all subconscious 'imprints' (*saṃskāra*) are shut down. It is superior to the 'concentration with seed' (*sabīja-samādhi*).[6]

§ C1-7 The Triad of Transformation
(= YS 3,9-15)

§ C1-2 The Transformation of the Shutdown
(= YS 3,9-10)

§ C1
= YS 3,9

व्युत्थाननिरोधसंस्कारयोरभिभवप्रादुर्भावौ निरोधक्षणचित्तान्वयो निरोधपरिणामः ।

vyutthāna-nirodha-saṃskārayor abhibhava-prādurbhāvau nirodha-kṣaṇa-cittânvayo nirodha-pariṇāmaḥ.

The overpowering (*abhibhava*) [of the 'imprint'] of activity (*vyutthāna*) and the appearance (*pradurbhāva*) of the 'imprint' (*saṃskāra*) of the shutdown (*nirodha*) are the transformation (*pariṇāma*) of the shutdown. It follows (*anvaya*) the thinking (*citta*) in the moment (*kṣaṇa*) of its shutdown.

§ C1 and the following six maxims try to explain what enables the yogī to perform the supernatural faculties, the siddhis (after he has shut down the movements of the

6 *nirbīja-samādhi* is mentioned in § E40 (=YS 1,51), *sabīja-samādhi* in § E35 (=YS 1,46).

thinking). The explanation starts with certain processes befalling his subconsciousness which commence with the appearance of a new kind of subconscious karma imprint (*saṃskāra*).

§ C1 answers the question what is about to happen directly after the shutdown of the movements of the thinking (the end of Part B). The answer is concerned with two different kinds of subconscious karma 'imprints' (*saṃskāra*). The first kind existed in activity (*vyutthāna*), as long as the thinking was still moving. This first kind of subconscious karma imprints was responsible for a person acting similarly over and over again in similar situations. By these actions, the person collected every new karma, and was therefore reincarnated.

This first kind of 'imprints' is now 'overpowered' (*abhibhava*, 'subjugation'). But now a novel kind of imprint appears, the imprint of the shutdown (*nirodha-saṃskāra*). The appearance of this novel imprint is called the 'transformation' (*pariṇāma*) of the shutdown of the movements of the thinking.

vyutthāna, the 'activity,' is the opposite pole to *samādhi*, 'concentration.'[7]

§ C2 तस्य प्रशान्तवाहिता संस्कारात् ।
= YS 3,10 *tasya praśānta-vāhitā saṃskārāt.*

Its calm flow by an[other] 'imprint.'

The 'calm flow' of this 'transformation' of the shutdown, i.e. the 'imprint' resulting directly from the shutdown of the movements of the thinking, is caused by another 'imprint.'

§ C3 The Transformation of the Concentration
(= YS 3,11)

§ C3 सर्वार्थतैकाग्रतयोः क्षयोदयौ चित्तस्य समाधिपरिणामः ।
= YS 3,11 *sarvârthatâikâgratayoḥ kṣayôdayau cittasya samādhi-pariṇāmaḥ.*

The disappearance of the condition in which all is object and the rise of the 'one-pointedness' (*ekâgratā*) of the thinking is the transformation of the 'concentration.'

In the state of 'concentration' (*samādhi*) 'all is object' (*sarva-artha-tā*). But this condition is now about to disappear. Instead, the thinking becomes 'one-pointed' (*eka-agra-tā*). Apparently it obtains an object again, if only one – and this routine is called the 'transformation of the concentration' (*samādhi-pariṇāma*).

sarvârthatâikâgratayoḥ is a dvandva compound in the genitive case, dependent on the following dvandva *kṣayôdayau*. In this construction, *kṣaya* relates to *sarvârthatā* and *udaya* to *ekâgratā*.

7 The term *vyutthāna* occurs elsewhere in the Yogasūtras, only in § C30 (=YS 3,38).

cittasya in the genitive case is in post-position.[8]

§ C4 The Transformation of the One-Pointedness
(= YS 3,12)

§ C4
= YS 3,12

ततः पुनः शान्तोदितौ तुल्यप्रत्ययौ चित्तस्यैकाग्रतापरिणामः ।

tataḥ punaḥ śāntôditau tulya-pratyayau cittasyâikāgratā-pariṇāmaḥ.

When then again the quietened and the [meanwhile newly] emerged 'concept' of thinking are equal, [then this is] the 'transformation of the one-pointedness.'

The quietened concept of thinking is that condition in which 'all is object', and the newly emerged concept of thinking is the 'one-pointedness.' When both concepts are equal, this is called the transformation of the one-pointedness. But these 'concepts' (*pratyaya*) are apparently not to be understood as a movement of the thinking, for – 'the "observer" is pure "observing". [He may be] pure, yet he observes by way of concepts.'[9]

§ C5-7 Addenda to the Triad of Transformation
(= YS 3,13-15)

§ C5
= YS 3,13

एतेन भूतेन्द्रियेषु धर्मलक्षणावस्थापरिणामा व्याख्याताः ।

etena bhūtendriyeṣu dharma-lakṣaṇâvasthā-pariṇāmā vyākhyātāḥ.

Thereby are already explained the transformations of the 'entity factors' (*dharmāḥ*), the characteristics and the state of the elements and the sense[10] organs.

Here and in the two following sūtras, I can only refer to parallel occurences of the terms.[11]

§ C6
= YS 3,14

शान्तोदिताव्यपदेश्यधर्मानुपाती धर्मी ।

śāntôditâvyapadeśya-dharmânupātī dharmī.

He who follows the quietened, emerged and not-to-be-defined 'entity factors,' has their peculiar properties.

8 Cf. the same construction in § P27 (=YS 3,1) and C31.

9 § P4 (=YS 2,20).

10 The activities of the five organs of sense are enumerated in § C29 (= YS 3,37).

11 As for *indriya* see the note on § P2 (=YS 2,18). – *dharma* in § D11 (=YS 4,12) is also in the plural. – *lakṣaṇa* occurs in the YS only here and in § C46 (=YS 3,54). – *avasthā* only here. *avasthāna* in § B3 (=YS 1,3). *anavasthitatva* in § B30 (=YS 1,30).

dharmin, 'having the properties of, having the nature, peculiar properties or characteristics of anything' (Apte) is another hapax (a word that occurs only once) in the Yogasūtras.

§ C7 = YS 3,15

क्रमान्यत्वं पारिणामान्यत्वे हेतुः ।
kramânyatvaṃ pariṇāmânyatve hetuḥ.

The difference in succession is the the reason for the difference in the transformation.

The three kinds of 'transformation' (i.e. of the shutdown of the movements of the thinking, of 'concentration' and of 'one-pointedness') differ from each other depending on how they follow each other. The meaning remains unclear.

|||

§ C8-49 The Supernatural Faculties (*siddhi*)

(= YS 3,16-[4,1]

§ C8 Recognition of Past and Future

(= YS 3,16)

§ C8 = YS 3,16

पारिणामत्रयसंयमादतीतानागतज्ञानम् ।
pariṇāma-traya-saṃyamād atîtânāgata-jñānam.

From the 'interconnection' (*saṃyama*) of the triad of transformation (*pariṇāma-traya*) results the recognition of past and future (*atîtânāgata-jñāna*).

§ C9 Recognition of the Roar of All Beings

(= YS 3,17)

§ C9 = YS 3,17

शब्दार्थप्रत्ययानामितरेतराध्यासात्संकरस्तत्प्रविभागसंयमात्सर्वभूतरुतज्ञानम् ।
śabdârtha-pratyayānām itarêtarâdhyāsāt saṃkaras tat-pravibhāga-saṃyamāt sarva-bhūta-ruta-jñānam.

From placing sound, object and concept one upon the other results a mixed confusion. From interconnecting (*saṃyama*) the fragmentation of [the parts of] this [mixture] results the recognition of the roar (*ruta*) of all beings.

bhūta does *not* mean 'element' here,[12] but 'being,' be it divine, human or animal.

12 *bhūta*, 'element,' in § P2 (=YS 2,18) and § C5 (=YS 3,13).

ruta, the 'roar' or just 'sound.' The word is etymologically related to Latin *rūmor*, with the basic meaning 'a muffled sound,' e. g. of oars. – Cf. the supernatural faculty of 'divine hearing' (*divya śrotra*).[13]

§ C10 Recognition of Previous Births
(= YS 3,18)

§ C10 = YS 3,18
संस्कारसाक्षात्करणात्पूर्वजातिज्ञानम् ।
saṃskāra-sākṣātkaraṇāt pūrva-jāti-jñānam.

From realising (*sākṣātkaraṇa*) the subconscious karma imprints results the recognition [of the kind] of previous births.[14]

The language usage here is purely Buddhist. The Buddhists call this recollection of one's own 'previous rebirths': 'the realising of the recognition of the recollection of previous births' (*pūrva-nivāsa-ânusmṛti-jñāna-sākṣātkriyā*). The relevant passage from the canon of the Dharmaguptaka school was translated in 412-413 AD from the Middle Indic language Gāndhārī into the Chinese. Being quite close to the Pāli and Sanskrit parallels, it illustrates the yogic miracle very nicely, too:

> ...Then he is able to recollect the various countless events in previous existences. He remembers one rebirth ... countless rebirths. He is able to recollect how many eras emerged and went by, how he died here and was born there, his name, family and class, whether his food had been good or bad, his span of living long or short, the sufferings and pleasures he felt, his looks, his appearance, – he remembers everything.[15]

§ C11 Mind Reading
(= YS 3,19-20)

§ C11 = YS 3,19
प्रत्ययस्य परचित्तज्ञानम् ।
pratyayasya para-citta-jñānam.

[From realising] the concept (*pratyaya*) [results] the recognition of others' thinking.

Cf. § C27.

§ C12 = YS 3,20
न च तत्सालम्बनं तस्याविषयीभूतत्वात् ।
na ca tat sâlambanaṃ tasyâviṣayībhūtatvāt.

13 In § C34 (=YS 3,42).

14 *jāti*, § B22 (=YS 2,13), § P15 (=YS 2,31).

15 Quoted from the author's edition and translation *Das Śrāmaṇyaphala-Sūtra*, 1987, p. 347.

But one does not [know] that which is dependent [on the thoughts of others] because it has not become [one's] sense object.

Bangali Baba, in his edition and translation of the Yogasūtras, together with Vyāsa's commentary (1976), has this and the following sūtra as only part of the commentary.

§ C13-14 Disappearance
(= YS3,21-22)

§ C13
= YS 3,21

कायरूपसंयमात्तद्ग्राह्यशक्तिस्तम्भे चक्षुःप्रकाशासंप्रयोगेऽन्तर्धानम् ।
kāya-rupa-saṃyamāt tad-grāhya-śakti-stambhe cakṣuḥ-prakāśâsaṃprayoge 'ntardhānam.

From [directing] the 'interconnection' (*saṃyama*) upon the shape of [one's own] body and blocking (*stambha*) one's (*tad-*) [own] 'perceivable' (*grāhya*) 'potency' (*śakti*) and disconnecting (*asaṃprayoga*) [oneself] from the radiation of the sense of sight (*cakṣus*) [of the other] results disappearance (or 'invisibility').

See p. 25.

§ C14
= YS 3,22

एतेन शब्दाद्यन्तर्धानमुक्तम् ।
etena śabdâdy-antardhānam uktam.

By this, the disappearance of sound etc. is [also] discussed.

If one disconnects oneself from others' 'sense of sight,'[16] the object of the sense of sight, i.e. the form or shape (*rūpa*) disappears. In order to let the remaining four kinds of sense objects (*viṣaya*) disappear too, one shall, in analogy, proceed and disconnect oneself from the others' sense of hearing, touch, taste and sense of smell.

B and H have this sūtra only as part of Vyāsa's commentary.

§ C15 Recognition of Death
(= YS 3,23)

§ C15
= YS 3,23

सोपक्रमं निरुपक्रमं च कर्म तत्संयमादपरान्तज्ञानमरिष्टेभ्यो वा ।
sôpakramaṃ nirupakramaṃ ca karma tat-saṃyamād aparânta-jñānam ariṣṭebhyo vā.

[The effects of] karma are either imminent or far-off. From [directing the technique of] 'interconnection' (*saṃyama*) upon this [karma and its effects] results the recognition of death (*aparânta*); or from bad omens.

16 *cakṣus*, § C13 (=YS 3,21).

§ C16-17 Strength
(= YS 3,24-25)

§ C16
= YS 3,24

मैत्र्यादिषु बलानि ।
maitry-ādiṣu balāni.

[From directing the technique of 'interconnection,' *saṃyama*] upon friendliness etc. result strengths.

'Friendliness etc.' is abbreviated for 'friendliness, compassion, pleasure and equanimity' (*maitrī, karuṇā, muditā* and *upekṣā*).[17]

§ C17
= YS 3,25

बलेषु हस्तिबलादीनि ।
baleṣu hasti-balâdīni.

[From directing the technique of 'interconnection,' *saṃyama*] upon the strengths [result] the strength of an elephant etc.

Of course this is wishful thinking according to the law of magic, known as *similia similibus*, 'similar effects by similar causes.' The underlying idea is that of an analogy of microcosm and macrocosm. What is done in the microcosm, must have its effects on a macrocosmic scale as well. Cf. § C21, C22 and C32.

§ C18 Recognition of Things Subtle, Hidden and Far-Off
(=YS 3,26)

§ C18
= YS 3,26

प्रवृत्त्यालोकन्यासात्सूक्ष्मव्यवहितविप्रकृष्टज्ञानम् ।
pravṛtty-āloka-nyāsāt sūkṣma-vyavahita-viprakṛṣṭa-jñānam.

From directing (*nyāsāt*) one's contemplation (*āloka*) upon activities results the recognition of things subtle, hidden and far-off.

nyāsa can also mean 'renunciation' or 'abstinence,' so one could (quite differently) translate, 'from abstaining from the contemplation of activities…'

The 'activities' (*pravṛtti*) are connected with objects of sense (*viṣaya*).[18]

17 See § B33 (=YS 1,33).

18 According to § B35 (=YS 1,35). *pravṛtti* occurs again in § D4 (=YS 4,5).

§ C19-21 Recognition of heavenly bodies
(=YS 3,27-29)

§ C19 भुवनज्ञानं सूर्ये संयमात्।
= YS 3,27 *bhuvana-jñānaṃ sūrye saṃyamāt.*

[From directing the technique of 'interconnection,' *saṃyama*] on the sun results the recognition of the world.

§ C20 चन्द्रे ताराव्यूहज्ञानम्।
= YS 3,28 *candre tārā-vyūha-jñānam.*

[From directing the technique of 'interconnection,' *saṃyama*] on the moon [results] the recognition of the arrangement of the stars.

vyūha does not mean 'totality' here, but rather 'arrangement.'[19]

§ C21 ध्रुवे तद्गतिज्ञानम्।
= YS 3,29 *dhruve tad-gati-jñānam.*

[From directing the technique of 'interconnection,' *saṃyama*] on the Pole Star [results] the recognition of their (i.e. the stars') course.

Polaris is the only star (which can be seen with the naked eye) that does not seem to move. That is why it is called Dhruva in Sanskrit, 'firm,' 'immovable.' All the other stars appear to circle around it. This obvious astronomical observation can easily lead to astrological identifications concerning the turns (*gati*) and motions of the stars around the astronomical north pole. This is again the magical association of *similia similibus*, as in § C17.

§ C22-27 Meditation on Parts of the Body
(=YS 3,30-35, except 3,34)

§ C22 नाभिचक्रे कायव्यूहज्ञानम्।
= YS 3,30 *nābhi-cakre kāya-vyūha-jñānam.*

[From directing the technique of 'interconnection,' *saṃyama*] upon the circle of the navel [results] the recognition of the overall arrangement[20] (*vyūha*) of the body.

Cf. the note on § C17.

19 See § C22 (=YS 3,30).

20 *vyūha*, § C20 (=YS 3,28).

§ C23
= YS 3,31

कण्ठकूपे क्षुत्पिपासानिवृत्तिः ।
kaṇṭha-kūpe kṣut-pipāsā-nivṛttiḥ.

[From directing the technique of 'interconnection,' *saṃyama*] upon the pit of the throat (precisely: the pit below the larynx) [results] the cessation of hunger and thirst.

nivṛttiḥ, the 'cessation,' is the antonym of *pravṛtti*, the activity.[21]

§ C24
= YS 3,32

कूर्मनाड्यां स्थैर्यम् ।
kūrma-nāḍyāṃ sthairyam.

[From *saṃyama*] upon the pulse [results] firmness.

kūrma-nāḍi (also *-nāḍī*), the 'vein of the turtle,' the pulse.

§ C25
= YS 3,33

मूर्धज्योतिषि सिद्धदर्शनम् ।
mūrdha-jyotiṣi Siddha-darśanam.

[From *saṃyama*] upon the light of the skull [results] the perception of the Perfected Ones (*Siddha*).

Or: ...a perception like the Perfected Ones.' The Siddhas are a class of divine beings or saints, possessing supernatural faculties or 'perfections' (*siddhi*). They are transferred into the air space after their death. See, for example, Kālidāsa's *Meghadūta*.[22]

§ C26
= YS 3,34

प्रातिभाद्वा सर्वम् ।
prātibhād vā sarvam.

Or from enlightenment[23] everything.

The Sanskrit poetology (Alaṃkāraśāstra) knows this figure of speech as *atiśaya*, 'exaggeration.'

§ C27
= YS 3,35

हृदये चित्तसंवित् ।
hṛdaye citta-saṃvit.

[From *saṃyama*] upon the heart, knowledge of the thinking.

21 *nivṛttiḥ*, again in § D29 (=YS 4,30). *pravṛtti*, § B35 (=YS 1,35), § C18 (=YS 3,26), § D4 (=YS 4,5).

22 Stanzas 1.14, 1.22, 1.48, 1.58, in my translation (*Kālidāsa: Wolkenbote*, 2024) the note on p. 61.

23 *prātibha* occurs again in § C29 (=YS 3,37).

That the heart was the seat of the thoughts is a widespread archaic speculation. '...according to primitive belief, the heart is the seat of the life energy [...] on a higher level, the heart is deemed the centre of the whole mental nature of a human being.' (A. Bertholet: *Wörterbuch der Religionen*, Stuttgart ^{3}1976, s. v. *Herz.*) '...since antiquity is considered as the seat of the feelings, the religious perceptions and the courage; Empedokles even thought that the power of thinking had its seat in it.' (*Philosophisches Wörterbuch*, by H. Schmidt/ G. Schickkoff, Stuttgart ^{18}1969, s. v. *Herz*).

This sūtra is either supplementing or contradicting § C11, where meditation, not on the heart, but on the 'concept' (*pratyaya*), shall make mindreading possible.

The term *saṃvid* occurs in the YS only here.

§ C28-29 Recognition of the Soul
(= YS 3,36-37)

§ C28
= YS 3,36

सत्त्वपुरुषयोरत्यन्तासंकीर्णयोः प्रत्ययाविशेषो भोगः परार्थात्स्वार्थसंयमात्पुरुषज्ञानम् ।
sattva-puruṣayor atyantâsaṃkīrṇayoḥ pratyayâviśeṣo bhogaḥ parârthāt svârtha-saṃyamāt puruṣa-jñānam.

Experience (*bhoga*) has no different concepts (*pratyaya*) of [the material quality of] 'benevolence' (*sattva*) and the soul (*puruṣa*), which are quite unmixed. From [directing the technique of 'interconnection,' *saṃyama*] upon the object 'matter,' off the object of the 'other' (*para* = *puruṣa*?) results the recognition of the soul (*puruṣa*).

§ C29
= YS 3,37

ततः प्रातिभश्रावणवेदनादर्शास्वादवार्त्ता जायन्ते ।
tataḥ prātibha-śrāvaṇa-vedanâdarśâsvāda-vārttā jāyante.

From this (scil. from the recognition of the soul, *puruṣa*), hearing,[24] sensing, seeing, tasting and smelling[25] – all being due to enlightenment – are born.

We have just heard[26] that not only 'hearing' etc., but 'everything results from "enlightenment" (*prātibha*).'

§ C30 Superhuman Faculties Are Disadvantages
(= YS 3,38)

§ C30
= YS 3,38

ते समाधावुपसर्गा व्युत्थाने सिद्धयः ।
te samādhāv upasargā vyutthāne siddhayaḥ.

24 Supernatural hearing, cf. § C9 (=YS 3,17) and § C34 (=YS 3,42).

25 *vārttā*, „Geruchsempfindung" (pw).

26 § C26 (=YS 3,34).

These [siddhis] are unfortunate add-ons[27] (*upasarga*) during 'concentration' (*samādhi*), [but] 'perfections' (*siddhi*) during activity.

'These' (siddhis) are the previously mentioned various kinds of supernatural recognition. They disturb the meditative 'concentration' (*samādhi*), but are supposed to enable the adept during his participation in the *vita activa* (*vyutthāna*) to acquire supernatural faculties, the siddhis. (This paragraph is a glosse, see p. 17.)

§ C31 Intrusion into others' bodies
(=YS 3,39)

§ C31
= YS 3,39

बन्धकारणशैथिल्यात्प्रचारसंवेदनाच्च चित्तस्य परशरीरावेशः ।
bandha-kāraṇa-śaithilyāt pracāra-saṃvedanāc ca cittasya para-śarī-râveśaḥ.

From the relaxation of the causes of fixation of the thinking[28] and the cumulative sensing (*saṃvedana*) of proceeding (*pracāra*), results the intrusion (*āveśa*) into others' bodies.

§ C32 Not-Clinging, and Breaking Even
(=YS 3,40)

§ C32
= YS 3,40

उदानजयाज्जलपङ्ककण्टकादिष्वसङ्ग उत्क्रान्तिश्च ।
udāna-jayāj jala-paṅka-kaṇṭakâdiṣv asaṅga utkrāntiś ca.

From conquering the 'breathing upwards' (*udāna*) results the not-clinging (*asaṅga*) to water, mud, thorns etc., and the breaking even.

We find the same kind of magical thinking here as in § C17, the *similia similibus*.
udāna, 'one of the five vital airs or life-winds which rises up the throat and enters into the head; the other four being *prāṇa*, *apāna*, *samāna* and *vyāna*' (Apte); „der sich von unten nach oben bewegende Wind im Körper" (pw).

§ C33 Burning by Overall Breathing
(=YS 3,41)

§ C33
= YS 3,41

समानजयाज्ज्वलनम् ।
samāna-jayāj jvalanam.

From conquering the 'overall breathing' (*samāna*) results burning.

27 *upasargāḥ* can even mean 'misfortunes,' 'calamities,' 'harms.'

28 Regarding the post-positioning of *cittasya* (in the genitive case), see § P27 (=YS 3,1) and § C3-4 (=YS 3,11-12).

samāna, the 'overall breathing,' 'one of the five life-winds or vital airs which has its seat in the cavity of the navel and is essential to digestion' (Apte).[29]

'Burning' means 'fire-breathing', cf. the notes on § C38.

§ C34 Divine Hearing
(=YS 3,42)

§ C34
= YS 3,42

श्रोत्राकाशयोः संबन्धसंयमाद् दिव्यं श्रोत्रम् ।

śrotrâkāśayoḥ saṃbandha-saṃyamād divyaṃ śrotram.

From [directing the technique of] 'interconnection' (*saṃyama*) upon the link between hearing and air space results 'divine hearing.'

As to other kinds of supernatural hearing, see § C9 (=YS 3,17) and § C29 (=YS 3,37).

§ C35 Walking through the Air
(=YS 3.43)

C 35
= YS 3,43

कायाकाशयोः संबन्धसंयमाल्लघुतूलसमापत्तेश्चाकाशगमनम् ।

kāyâkāśayoḥ saṃbandha-saṃyamāl laghu-tūla-samāpatteś câkāśa-gamanam.

From [directing the technique of] 'interconnection' (*saṃyama*) upon the link between body and air space and from the 'unification' (*samāpatti*) with light cotton, results walking through the air.

§ C36 The Disappearance of the Veil over the Inward Light
(=YS [3,44])

§ C36
= YS [3,44]

बहिरकल्पिता वृत्तिर्महाविदेहा ततः प्रकाशावरणक्षयः ।

bahir akalpitā vṛttir mahā-videhā tataḥ prakāśâvaraṇa-kṣayaḥ.

The movement [of the thinking] which is not endowed with outward imaginations is the 'great immaterialisation.' This results in the disappearance of the veil over the [inward] light.

There are many reasons to consider this sūtra as spurious, see p. 25.

29 See § C32 (=YS 3,40).

§ C37-39 Conquering the elements
(=YS 3,45-47)

§ C37
= YS 3,45

स्थूलस्वरूपसूक्ष्मान्वयार्थवत्त्वसंयमाद् भूतजयः ।
sthūla-sva-rūpa-sūkṣmânvayârthavattva-saṃyamād bhūta-jayaḥ.

By [directing the technique of 'interconnection,' *saṃyama*] upon how the coarse, the matter and the subtle follow each other and which objects they have, one conquers the elements.

sva-rūpa, lit. that which has the shape of the matter, as in Part B.[30] But here it has a different meaning, taking the middle position between the course and the subtle. Perhaps it means something like raw material, which becomes either subtle or coarse. The coarse is – as opposed to the subtle – unfolded (*vyakta*) and therefore visible.[31]

§ C38
= YS 3,46

ततोऽणिमादिप्रादुर्भावः कायसंपत्तद्धर्मानभिघातश्च ।
tato 'ṇimâdi-prādur-bhāvaḥ kāya-saṃpat tad-dharmânabhighātaś ca.

From this (what is described in § C37) emerges extreme diminutiveness (*aṇiman*) etc. (or: from this emerges the faculty to make oneself extremely small etc.), moreover the excellence of the body and the inviolability[32] of its 'entity factors' (*dharmāḥ*).[33]

aṇiman can be interpreted here in a double sense. Either it means the ability to perceive even the tiniest atom, *aṇu*, 'the smallest perceptible quantity' (Apte). Or, on the other hand, *aṇiman* is „die Zauberkraft sich unendlich klein zu machen" (pw, 'the witchery to make oneself infinitely small'). *-ādi*, 'etc.,' in that case means analogous witcheries, e. g. to make oneself extremely big.

To make oneself invisible, or extremely small, is opposed to being able to touch the sun and moon with one's hand. This is also considered by the Buddhists as a supernatural faculty. Buddhist texts mention more conjuring tricks, e. g. to manifold oneself, to walk through walls, to sink into the earth, to walk on the water and to bodily reach the Brahma world, even fire-breathing or the ability to pass enormous amounts of water.[34]

§ C39
= YS 3,47

रूपलावण्यबलवज्रसंहननत्वानि कायसंपत् ।

30 § B3 (=YS 1,3).

31 According to § D12 (=YS 4,13).

32 *anabhighāta* occurred already in § P19 (=YS 2,48); there, it was about the 'inviolability' or conflict of contradictions (*dvandva*).

33 As to *dharmāḥ*, see the commentary on § C5f (=YS 3,13f).

34 See the author's: *Das Śrāmaṇyaphala-Sūtra*, 1987, pp. 336f.

rūpa-lāvaṇya-bala-vajra-saṃhananatvāni kāya-saṃpat.

Beauty, grace, strength and diamond-hardness are the excellence of the body.

This is an additional comment on the preceding § C38.

§ C40-41 Conquering the Sense Organs
(=YS 3,48-49)

§ C40
= YS 3,48

ग्रहणस्वरूपास्मितान्वयार्थवत्त्वसंयमादिन्द्रियजयः ।

grahaṇa-sva-rūpâsmitânvayârthavattva-saṃyamād indriya-jayaḥ.

By [directing the technique of 'interconnection,' *saṃyama*] upon – on the one hand – 'perceiving' (*grahaṇa*) and – on the other hand – how the thoughts (*sva-rūpa*) and egocentricity follow each other and that [egocentricity] has an object, one conquers the sense[35] organs.

Soul and matter, the two different categories, shall both simultaneously become an object of meditation. However, 'perceiving' (*grahaṇa*)[36] is a function of the *soul* in the state of the *unio mystica*, during the 'unification' (*samāpatti*) of percipient, perceiving and the perceivable. Thoughts and egocentricity[37], on the other hand, belong to the area of the *matter*. The author of this sūtra depends heavily on the maker of Part B, the 'imitator.' But he ignores the strict and exclusive dualism of the latter's philosophical system.

§ C41
= YS 3,49

ततो मनोजवित्वं विकरणभावः प्रधानजयश्च ।

tato mano-javitvaṃ vikaraṇa-bhāvaḥ pradhāna-jayaś ca.

From this (i.e. the conquering of the sense organs, § C40) [results] swiftness of the mind, the condition of modifying, and conquering the primeval matter.

The 'primeval matter' (*pradhāna*), only occurs in the YS here. It appears to be another term for the 'matter.'[38]

35 The activities of the five organs of sense are enumerated in § C29 (= YS 3,37).

36 *grahaṇa*, only occurs elsewhere in the YS in § B41 (=YS 1,41).

37 § B15 (= YS 2,6).

38 *pradhāna*, 'the first [...] source of the material world, the primary germ out of which all material appearances are evolved, according to Sāṃkhya philosophy' (Apte). And similarly Vyāsa's commentary: *sarva-prakṛti-vikāra-vaśitvaṃ pradhāna-jayaḥ*, 'conquering *pradhāna* [means] the power to modify (*vikāra*) the whole of the *prakṛti*.' (*vikāra* and *vikaraṇa* are synonymous.)

§ C42-44 (=YS [3,50-52]) Isolation as a Supernatural Faculty

§ C42 = YS 3,50
सत्त्वपुरुषान्यताख्यातिमात्रस्य सर्वभावाधिष्ठातृत्वं सर्वज्ञातृत्वं च ।
sattva-puruṣânyatā-khyāti-mātrasya sarva-bhāvâdhiṣṭhātṛtvaṃ sarva-jñātṛtvaṃ ca.

In him who only perceives the difference between 'benevolence' (*sattva*) and the 'soul' (*puruṣa*), [arises] loftiness above all being and omniscience.

§ C42-44 (=YS 3,50-52) and § C48 (=YS 3,56) belong together and are obviously of a spurious nature, see p. 25.

§ C43 = YS 3,51
तद्वैराग्यादपि दोषबीजक्षये कैवल्यम् ।
tad-vairāgyād api doṣa-bīja-kṣaye kaivalyam.

Even from dispassion towards this (viz. the perception of the difference of benevolence and soul) and from when the seed of the failures has vanished, results 'isolation' (of the soul).

§ C42-44 (=YS 3,50-3,52) contain addenda to 'isolation,' scil. isolation of the soul by abandoning the conjunction between soul and matter. Here, in addition, isolation is deemed a supernatural faculty (*siddhi*).

doṣa, 'mistake,' 'failure,' one of the three main evils according to the teaching of the Buddha, only occurs in the Yogasūtras here. The term appears to have been of minor concern in the yoga tradition.

§ C44 = YS 3,52
स्थान्युपनिमन्त्रणे सङ्गस्मयाकरणं पुनरनिष्टप्रसङ्गात् ।
sthāny-upanimantraṇe saṅga-smayâkaraṇaṃ punar-aniṣṭa-prasaṅgāt.

When one is invited by 'him who stands fast' one should refrain from sympathy and pride, in order to not be attached again to the non-desirable.

All terms used in this sūtra only occur in the Yogasūtras here. Therefore, the meaning must remain in the dark. Nevertheless, I allow myself to speculate:

- 'He who stands fast' (*sthānī*) is yet another term for the soul.
- The 'invitation' (*nimantraṇa*) refers to the 'unification' with the soul.[39]
- The invitation is directed towards the meditating yogī.
- The 'non-desirable' is the state of the unenlightened worldling.

39 According to § B41 or § P29.

§ C45-47 Knowledge Born from Discrimination|||
(= YS 3,53-55)

§ C45 क्षणतत्क्रमयोः संयमाद्विवेकजं ज्ञानम् ।
= YS 3,53 *kṣaṇa-tat-kramayoḥ saṃyamād viveka-jaṃ jñānam.*

From [directing the technique of 'interconnection,' *saṃyama*] upon the moments and their succession, results knowledge born from discrimination.

§ C46 जातिलक्षणदेशैरन्यतानवच्छेदात्तुल्ययोस्ततः प्रतिपत्तिः ।
= YS 3,54 *jāti-lakṣaṇa-deśair anyatânavacchedāt tulyayos tataḥ pratipattiḥ.*

From this arises cognisance of two [items] that are equal because they are not delimited by (and therefore independent from) a difference of birth,[40] a distinctive mark and place.

§ C47 तारकं सर्वविषयं सर्वथाविषयमक्रमं चेति विवेकजं ज्ञानम् ।
= YS 3,55 *tārakaṃ sarva-viṣayaṃ sarvathā-viṣayam akramaṃ cêti viveka-jaṃ jñānam.*

Helping to cross over, having everything as its object, having objects in every respect and without order (or sequence): such is the recognition born from discrimination.

§ C48 Benevolence of the Soul
(= YS [3,56]

§ C48 सत्त्वपुरुषयोः शुद्धिसाम्ये कैवल्यम् ।
= YS 3,56 *sattva-puruṣayoḥ śuddhi-sāmye kaivalyam.*

When the soul is as pure as the benevolence (*sattva*), it is 'isolation.'

I also hesitated to ascribe this paragraph to the 'conjurer.' But it uses the same terminology as § C42 (cf. p. 25). And it makes a grandiose finale for the whole Part C.

40 *jāti*, § P15 (=YS 2,31).

Part D

Miscellanies

§ D1-33 (=YS 4,2-34)

Part D consists mostly of enigmatic materials that have little to do with what we have heard in the first three parts. The remarks collected here are late additions by an anonymous revisor and editor. He was reluctant to neglect any teachings accumulated in the Indian yoga scene of about the first half of the first millennium AD. I would like to call him the 'gatherer.'

§ D1-2 (=YS 4,2-3) Cutting off the Transformation into Birth

§ D1 = YS 4,2

जत्यन्तरपरिणामः प्रकृत्यापूरात् ।

jāty-antara-pariṇāmaḥ prakṛty-āpūrāt.

The transformation[1] into birth arises from the abundance of the matter (*prakṛti*).

This maxim is related to § E19 which reads: 'There is a concept of rebirth of those ['souls,' *puruṣa*] who are immaterially dissolved in the 'matter' (*prakṛti*).'

§ D2 = YS 4,3

निमित्तमप्रयोजकं प्रकृतीनां वरणभेदस्तु ततः क्षेत्रिकवत् ।

nimittam aprayojakaṃ prakṛtīnāṃ varaṇa-bhedas tu tataḥ kṣetrika-vat.

The cause (*nimitta*) [of rebirth] (i.e. the soul) is not connected with the basic forms (or: elements) of the matter.[2] The cutting off of [its] obstacles, however, [is done] by it (the soul) – as if [by] a peasant.

'...is done by the soul.' The soul cuts off the obstacles of transformation into rebirth, 'like a peasant,' the weeds. The peasant represents the soul. The weeds must be added, due to the extremely abbreviated diction of the sūtra. They are a metaphor for the basic forms of the matter.

1 *pariṇāma*, cf. § B24 (=YS 2,15) and § C7-8 (=YS 3,15-16).

2 *prakṛtīnāṃ*, 'the eight primary elements out of which everything else is evolved,' or 'the five primary elements of creations (*pañca-mahābhūtāni*)' (Apte, for *prakṛti* in the plural); „die materiellen Grundformen" (pw).

§ D3-10 Thoughts of Rebirth
(=YS 4,4-11)

§ D3
= YS 4,4

निर्माणचित्तान्यस्मितामात्रात् ।
nirmāṇa-cittāny asmitā-mātrāt.

Thoughts of creation arise only through egocentricity.

nirmāṇa-cittāni, 'thoughts of creation.' Based on the Buddhist understanding of *nirmāṇa-kāya*, 'body of magic transformation' (BHSD), one can translate *nirmāṇa-cittāni* here as 'thoughts of rebirth.'

§ D4
= YS 4,5

प्रवृत्तिभेदे प्रयोजकं चित्तमेकमनेकेषाम् ।
pravṛtti-bhede prayojakaṃ cittam ekam anekeṣām.

When [the soul] cuts (*bheda*) off the thought [of returning] into activity,[3] [this] single thought [will remain] connected with the many [others].

§ D5
= YS 4,6

तत्र ध्यानजमनाशयम् ।
tatra dhyāna-jam anāśayam.

In this respect, [thoughts] born by meditation (*dhyāna*) are free from [subconscious karma] 'dispositions.'[4]

§ D6
= YS 4,7

कर्माशुक्लाकृष्णं योगिनस्त्रिविधमितरेषाम् ।
karmâśuklâkṛṣṇaṃ yoginas trividham itareṣām.

The karma of a yogī is neither white nor black. Threefold [is the karma] of the others.

The karma of the worldling (*itara*) is either white or black or mixed white and black, which means that it is either affected by joy (*sukha*) or by suffering (*duḥkha*) or by a mixture of both. Only the accomplished yogī does not collect karma anymore. Thus, he can avoid rebirth. The idea is adopted from Buddhism, it forms the core of the 'Sūtra of the Four Classes.'[5]

3 *pravṛtti*, cf. § B35 (=YS 1,35), § C18 (=YS 3,26). Cf. also P. Deussen: *Allgemeine Geschichte der Philosophie*, 1914, p. 537.

4 See the explanations of the subconscious karma 'dispositions' in § B21 (=YS 2,12) and § E24 (=YS 1,24).

5 See the author's: *Das Sūtra von den vier Ständen*, 1988, pp. 156-165 and 43, especially the *English Summary*, pp. 67-71.

§ D7 तसस्तद्विपाकानुगुणानामेवाभिव्यक्तिर्वासनानाम् ।
= YS 4,8
tatas tad-vipākânuguṇānām evâbhivyaktir vāsanānām.

That is why only those karma impressions (*vāsanā*) become unfolded (*abhivyakti*) [and therefore visible] which correspond (*anuguṇa*) to the maturation (*vipāka*) out of it (scil. out of their respective karma).

§ D8 जातिदेशकालव्यवहितानामप्यानन्तर्यं स्मृतिसंस्कारयोरेकरूपत्वात् ।
= YS 4,9
jāti-deśa-kāla-vyavahitānām apy ānantaryaṃ smṛti-saṃskārayor eka-rūpatvāt.

There is an uninterrupted succession of those [karma impressions] too, which are distinct (*vyavahita*) by birth, place and time, because [with regard to them] mindfulness and [subconscious karma] 'imprints' have the same form.

Because mindfulness and karma impressions have the same form, by way of the meditation technique of mindfulness (*smṛti*), the subconscious karma 'impressions' (*vāsanā*) and the karma 'imprints' caused by them can be made conscious.

§ D9 तासामनादित्वं चाशिषो नित्यत्वात् ।
= YS 4,10
tāsām anāditvaṃ câśiṣo nityatvāt.

And these [subconscious karma impressions] are without beginning, on account of the eternity of blessing.

The subconscious karma impressions bless – in a manner of speaking – themselves, which means that they make themselves permanent and thus operative for the next reincarnation. Vyāsa comments that this blessing (themselves) manifests itself by the desire to live. According to the cyclic worldview, this wheel of karma has no beginning – therefore it is eternal.

§ D10 हेतुफलाश्रयालम्बनैः संगृहीतत्वादेषामभावे तदभावः ।
= YS 4,11
hetu-phalâśrayâlambanaiḥ saṃgṛhītatvād eṣām abhāve tad-abhāvaḥ.

On account of the correlation between cause (*hetu*) and effect (*phala*), and between basis (*āśraya*) and support (*ālambana*), if those (i.e. cause and basis) do not exist, neither do these (i.e. effect and support) exist.

But if the causes and bases of the karma are removed, it cannot lean on them and produce effects.

§ D11-13 The 'Entity Factors' (*dharmāḥ*) and Their Relevance for the Reincarnation

(=YS 4,12-14)

§ D11
= YS 4,12

अतीतानगतं स्वरूपतोऽस्ति अध्वभेदाद्धर्माणाम् ।

atītânāgatam sva-rūpato 'sti adhva-bhedād dharmāṇām.

Items of the past and the future come into existence out of the thoughts (*sva-rūpa*, lit. that which has the shape of the matter)[6] because the 'entity factors' (*dharmāḥ*) break new ground.

This is possible because the entity factors are said to be inviolable.[7]

§ D12
= YS 4,13

ते व्यक्तसूक्ष्मा गुणात्मानः ।

te vyakta-sūkṣmā guṇâtmānaḥ.

They (viz. the 'entity factors') may be unfolded (*vyakta*) [and therefore visible] or subtle, their innermost essence (*ātman*) is their material qualities.[8]

§ D13
= YS 4,14

परिणामैकत्वाद्वस्तुतत्त्वम् ।

pariṇāmâikatvād vastu-tattvam.

From the unity of the transformation[9] results the reality (*tattva*) of the objects.

§ D14-30 Correlations between thought, object and soul

(=YS 4,15-31)

§ D14
= YS 4,15

वस्तुसाम्ये चित्तभेदात्तयोर्विभक्तः पन्थाः ।

vastu-sāmye citta-bhedāt tayor vibhaktaḥ panthāḥ.

In case of the equality [of two] objects, on account of the difference (*bheda*) of the thinking, the way of them both (viz. object and thinking) is divided.

6 Cf. § B3 (=YS 1,3).

7 According to § C38 (=YS 3,46) the 'entity factors' are inviolable. See also note on § C6 (=YS 3,14).

8 As to the 'material qualities' (*guṇa*) see § P2 (=YS 2,18).

9 *pariṇāma*, § C1-7 (=YS 3,9-15).

§ D15
= YS 4,16

न चैकचित्ततन्त्रं वस्तु तदप्रमाणकं तदा किं स्यात्

na câika-citta-tantraṃ vastu tad apramāṇakaṃ tadā kiṃ syāt.

And there is no object (*vastu*) that would be textured [only] by one thinking. This is unprovable. [For if it would exist] what would it be then?

The thinking (*citta*) encapsulates the object (*vastu*). Each object, however, is encapsulated by more than one thinking, though this is unprovable. To hypothesise only *one* thinking, would result in solipsism which is irreconcilable with the axiom of the multiplicity of souls.

§ D16
= YS 4,17

तदुपरागागापेक्षित्वाच्चित्तस्य वस्तु ज्ञाताज्ञातम्।

tad-uparāgâpekṣitvāc cittasya vastu jñātâjñātam.

An object (*vastu*) is recognised (*jñāta-*) by the thinking (*cittasya*), or not recognised (*-ajñātam*): it depends on how (*-apekṣitvāc*) [the thinking] colours (*uparāga-*)[10] it (*tad*, the object).

§ D17
= YS 4,18

सदा ज्ञातश्चित्तवृत्तयस्तत्प्रभोः पुरुषस्यापरिणामित्वात्।

sadā jñātāś citta-vṛttayas tat-prabhoḥ puruṣasyâpariṇāmitvāt.

The movements of the thinking are always recognised by their lord (*prabhu*), on account of the non-transformation of the soul (*puruṣa*).

Torturous[11] transformation (*pariṇāma*) which is a preposition to reincarnation, happens in the area of the matter (*prakṛti*). That is why the soul (*puruṣa, prabhu*) has no part in it. The soul, however, recognises the movements of the thinking which must be shut down to enable the soul to firmly stand in the middle of the matter, yet apart from it and thus becomes distinguishable from the movements of the thinking.[12]

§ D18
= YS 4,19

न तत्स्वाभासं दृश्यत्वात्।

na tat-svâbhāsaṃ dṛśyatvāt.

It (the soul) does not radiate (*ābhāsa*) materially (*sva*) because the [radiating belongs to the] 'matter.'

10 As to *uparāga* cf. *uparakta* in § D22 (=YS 4,23). Cf. also the term 'hue' (*añjanatā*) in § B41 (=YS 1,41).

11 *tāpa*, § B24 (=YS 2,15).

12 § B3 (=YS 1,3).

tat, 'it,' i.e. *prabhu*, the soul, also termed *svāmin*, *draṣṭṛ*, *puruṣa*, etc., according to the respective yogic movement which has found its way into the vulgate of the Yogasūtras.[13]

'Radiation' (*ābhāsa*) occurs in the Yogasūtras at three places:

• (1) '...only the 'sense' (*artha*) radiates (*nirbhāsa*), which is, as it were, devoid of that which has the shape of the 'matter' (*sva-rūpa*), – *sva-rūpa-śūnyêvârtha-mātra-nirbhāsā*.'[14]

• (2) '...only the object is radiating (*nirbhāsa*) and... it is – as it were – devoid of that which has the shape of the matter. – ...*artha-mātra-nirbhāsaṃ sva-rūpa-śūnyam iva*.'[15]

• (3) '...disconnecting (*asaṃprayoga*) [oneself] from the radiation (*prakāśa*) of the sense of sight (*cakṣus*).'[16]

All the three occurrences corroborate the statement of our paragraph here that 'the [radiating belongs to the] "matter".'

§ D19 एकसमये चोभयानवधारणम् ।
= YS 4,20 *eka-samaye côbhayânavadhāraṇam.*

And one does not keep hold of both at the same time.

Or: '...one does not perceive both...,' (*ubhaya*), 'both,' viz. thinking and object.[17]

§ D20 चित्तान्तरदृश्ये बुद्धिबुद्धेरतिप्रसङ्गः स्मृतिसंकरश्च ।
= YS 4,21 *cittântara-dṛśye buddhi-buddher atiprasaṅgaḥ smṛti-saṃkaraś ca.*

If I [can] see[18] the interior of [another person's] mind (*citta*), [then] [my] intelligence (*buddhi*) is too closely connected with the other. And there is a contamination of [mine and the other's] mindfulness (*smṛti*).

13 See notes on § B3 where I have listed the instances of the terms for 'soul.'

14 § E32 (=YS 1,43).

15 § P29 (=YS 3,3).

16 § C13 (=YS 3,21).

17 § D16 (=YS 4,17).

18 § C11 (=YS 3,19) discusses 'the recognition of others' thinking,' i.e. mind reading. Cf. also § C27 (=YS 3,35).

§ D21 चितेरप्रतिसंक्रमायास्तदाकारापत्तौ स्वबुद्धिसंवेदनम् ।
= YS 4,22 *citer apratisaṃkramāyās tad-ākārâpattau sva-buddhi-saṃvedanam.*

When the awareness (*citi*) does not stride up and down and when one perceives (*āpatti*) its shape (*ākāra*), then one senses that the intelligence (*buddhi*) [belongs to the area] of the 'matter' (*sva*).

Awareness is classified as a 'potency' (*śakti*).[19] Therefore it must belong to the material side (*sva*), together with the 'thinking' (*citta*) and the 'intelligence' (*buddhi*).

§ D22 द्रष्टृदृश्योपरक्तं चित्तं सर्वार्थम् ।
= YS 4,23 *draṣṭṛ-dṛśyôparaktaṃ cittaṃ sarvârtham.*

'Thinking' (*citta*) that is dyed (*uparakta*) by the 'observer' (*draṣṭṛ*, the soul) and the 'observable' (*dṛśya*, the matter) has everything[20] as its object (*artha*).

And thus it makes mind reading[21] possible.

§ D23 तदसंख्येयवासनाभिश्चित्रमपि परार्थं संहत्यकारित्वात् ।
= YS 4,24 *tad asaṃkhyeya-vāsanābhiś citram api parârthaṃ saṃhatya-kāritvāt.*

This, although multicoloured by countless [karma] 'impressions,' is directed to [the mind] of another [person] because of the co-operation.

'Co-operation' (*saṃhatya-kāritva*) can only refer to the co-action of the 'observer' (*draṣṭṛ = puruṣa*) and the 'observable' (*dṛśya = prakṛti*).[22]

§ D24 विशेषदर्शिन आत्मभावभावनाविनिवृत्तिः ।
= YS 4,25 *viśeṣa-darśina ātma-bhāva-bhāvanā-vinivṛttiḥ.*

He who observes the distinction (between 'seer,' *draṣṭṛ* and 'thinking,' *citta*) does not create (*bhāvanā*) the being of a 'self' (*ātman*) any more (*vinivṛtti*).

This paragraph is a very late interpolation. See p. 25.

19 In § D33 (=YS 4,34).

20 *sarva*, cf. § C26 (=YS 3,34) and § C42 (=YS 3,50). Cf. also § P1 (=YS 2,17).

21 § D20 (=YS 4,21).

22 § D22 (=YS 4,23).

§ D25 तदा हि विवेकनिम्नं कैवल्यप्राग्भारं चित्तम्।
= YS 4,26 *tadā hi viveka-nimnaṃ kaivalya-prāg-bhāraṃ cittam.*

Because (*hi*) from that moment onwards (*tadā*)[23] the thinking is deep in discrimination and high in 'isolation.'

§ D26 तच्छिद्रेषु प्रत्ययान्तराणि संस्कारेभ्यः।
= YS 4,27 *tac-chidreṣu pratyayântarāṇi saṃskārebhyaḥ.*

In its gaps (i.e. in the blank spaces of the 'thinking') [emerge] intervals (?) of concepts [caused] by the subconscious 'imprints' (*saṃskāra*).

§ D27 हानमेषां क्लेशवदुक्तम्।
= YS 4,28 *hānam eṣāṃ kleśa-vad uktam.*

How to get rid of these [subconscious karma 'imprints'] has been explained:[24] in the same way as of the 'defilements' (*kleśa*).

§ D28 प्रसंख्यानेऽप्यकुसीदस्य सर्वथा विवेकख्यातेर्धर्ममेघः समाधिः।
= YS 4,29 *prasaṃkhyāne 'py akusīdasya sarvathā viveka-khyāter dharma-meghaḥ samādhiḥ.*

In him who does not become indolent even during the [meditative technique of] prasaṃkhyāna (?), and who discriminates (*viveka-khyāti*) in every respect, arises the 'concentration with dharma clouds.' (?)

§ D29 ततः क्लेशकर्मनिवृत्तिः।
= YS 4,30 *tataḥ kleśa-karma-nivṛttiḥ.*

From this results the cessation of the defiling karma.[25]

§ D30 तदा सर्वावरणमलापेतस्य ज्ञानस्यानन्त्याज्ज्ञेयमल्पम्।
= YS 4,31 *tadā sarvâvaraṇa-malâpetasya jñānasyânantyāj jñeyam alpam.*

From that moment on, for him who is devoid of all encrustations (*āvaraṇa*) and blemishes (*mala*), because of the infinity of recognition [there will remain] little to be recognised.

23 As to *tadā*, 'from that moment on,' see my notes on § B3 (=YS 1,3). The same conjunction appears also in § D15 (= YS 4,16) and § D30 (=YS 4,31).

24 In § B19-20 (=YS 2,10-11), cf. also § E3 (=YS 2,2).

25 *kleśa-karman* also in § E24 (=YS 1,24).

§ D31-33 The End
(=YS 4,32-34)

§ D31
= YS 4,32

ततः कृतार्थानां परिणामक्रमसमाप्तिर्गुणानाम् ।

tataḥ kṛtârthānāṃ pariṇāma-krama-samāptir guṇānām.

Thereby [one arrives at] the end (*samāpti*) of the series (*krama*) of transformations[26] of the qualities[27] [of 'matter'] that have accomplished their aim.

§ D32
= YS 4,33

क्षणप्रतियोगी परिणामापरान्तनिर्ग्राह्यः क्रमः ।

kṣaṇa-pratiyogī pariṇāmâparânta-nirgrāhyaḥ kramaḥ.

The series (*krama*) [of transformations] corresponds (*pratiyogin*) to the moments (*kṣaṇa*) and is not perceivable at the extreme end of the transformations.

§ D33
= YS 4,34

पुरुषार्थशून्यानां गुणानां प्रतिप्रसवः कैवल्यं स्वरूपप्रतिष्ठा वा चितिशक्तेरिति ।

puruṣârtha-śūnyānāṃ guṇānāṃ pratiprasavaḥ kaivalyaṃ sva-rūpa-pratiṣṭhā vā citi-śakter iti.

The retrogression (*pratiprasava*) of the material qualities which are devoid of the object 'soul' (*puruṣa*), is 'isolation' (*kaivalya*). Or that the potency 'consciousness' (*citi*) stands still in the middle of the thoughts (*sva-rūpa*). – THE END.

The 'consciousness' (*citi*) belongs to the 'potency' (*śakti*) of the 'matter,'[28] similar to the 'thinking' (*citta*), as already stated at the beginning of Part B, which has also become, in the course of transmission, the beginning of the whole text of the vulgate.[29] The unknown editor or revisor who is responsible for adding this last sutra, and probably the whole of Part D tries to close the gap between the beginning and the end of the vulgate by referring to the phrase *draṣṭuḥ sva-rūpe 'vasthānam*. He replaces *avasthāna* by *pratiṣṭhā* however.

The conjunction *atha* was the first word at the very beginning of the Yogasūtras, *iti* concludes them.

26 *pariṇāma*, § C1-7 (=YS 3,9-15).

27 *guṇa*, § E29 (=YS 1,16).

28 In § D21 (=YS 4,22).

29 In § B3 (=YS 1,3).

Part E

The Extras

Minor Interpolations

§ E1-3 (=YS 2,32; 2,1-2); § E4-16 (= YS 2,33-45); § E17-22 (=YS 1,17-22); § E23-28 (=YS 1,23-28); § E29-30 (=YS 1,16-17); § E31-40 (=YS 1,42-51)

Part E contains late and minor additions which are scattered all over the text of Parts P and B of the Yogasūtras. These spurious sprinklings are presented here in an 'extra' part, to make it clear that they did not yet belong to the ancient text of Patañjali's Part P, nor to the imitator's reproductions in Part B. As a result, the 'extras' appear here in Part E devoid of any context.

The relevant text-critical explanations why these minor interpolations were added at their specific places, in a more or less fitting context, are given in the introductory chapter on textual criticism. I have provided the cross-references (from Part E to the chapter on textual criticism) in the notes below the respective sūtra.

The extras are organised in sub-chapters called 'The Yoga of Action,' 'Creation of the Opposite,' 'Postscript to the Shutdown,' 'Devotion to the God,' 'Dispassion Supreme,' 'Additions to the Unification,' and 'Birth, Drugs, Mantras, Austerities and Concentration.'

§ E1-3 The Yoga of Action
(=YS 2,32; 2,1-2)

§ E1
(an increase of § P16 = YS 2,32)

शौचसंतोषतपःस्वाध्यायेश्वरप्रणिधानानि नियमाः ।

śauca-saṃtoṣa-tapaḥ-svâdhyāyêśvara-praṇidhānāni niyamāḥ.

Purity and contentedness, (and also) penance, private studies and devotion to the god are the moral precepts.

Part E begins with the short interpolation of the *yoga of action.* The words 'purity and contentedness... are the moral precepts,' still belong to § P16, but 'penance, private studies and devotion to the god' are a late addition, an interpolation caused by the following two sūtras E2-3 (=YS 2,1-2). (See the textual criticism on p. 18.)

§ E2
= YS 2,1

तपःस्वाध्यायेश्वरप्रणिधानानि क्रियायोगः ।

tapaḥ-svâdhyāyêśvara-praṇidhānāni kriyā-yogaḥ.

Penance, private studies and devotion to the god are the yog*a of action.*

§ E3
= YS 2,2

समाधिभावनार्थः क्लेशतनूकरणार्थश्च ।
samādhi-bhāvanârthaḥ kleśa-tanūkaraṇârthaś ca.

(The *yoga of action*) aims at the meditative creation of 'concentration' (*samādhi*) and the 'thinning out' (*tanū-karaṇa*) of the 'defilements' (*kleśa*).

For the reasons of the interpolation of the paragraphs E2 and E3, see p. 18.

§ E4-16 The Creation of the Opposite (*pratipakṣa-bhāvana*)
(= YS 2,33-45)

§ E4
= YS 2,33

वितर्कबाधने प्रतिपक्षभावनम् ।
vitarka-bādhane pratipakṣa-bhāvanam.

If there is an obstacle to 'calculating' (*vitarka*), 'creation of the opposite' [is recommended].

See p. 22.

Two other techniques of meditation are called *bhāvana*, 'creation' (literally 'letting or making something become'), namely the muttering of the syllable *om*[1] and friendliness, compassion, pleasure and equanimity (*maitrī*, *karuṇā*, *muditā* and *upekṣā*).[2]

§ E5
= YS 2,34

वितर्का हिंसादयः कृतकारितानुमोदिता लोभक्रोधमोहपूर्वका मृदुमध्याधिमात्रा दुःखाज्ञानानन्तफला इति प्रतिपक्षभावनम् ।
vitarkā hiṃsâdayaḥ kṛta-kāritânumoditā lobha-krodha-moha-pūrvakā mṛdu-madhyâdhimātrā duḥkhâjñānânanta-phalā iti pratipakṣa-bhāvanam.

'Calculations' on violence etc., be them done, instigated or approved of, which are preceded by greed, anger and delusion, be them mild, middle or excessive, result in endless suffering and non-perception. In that case, the 'creation of the opposite' [is recommended].

'Violence etc.,' means the prohibited immoral ways of conduct: violence, falsehood, stealing, unchastity and 'clinging.'[3]

Greed, anger and delusion (*lobha-krodha-moha*) are the three fundamental evils disapproved of by the Buddha.

1 § E28 (=YS 1,28).

2 § B33 (=YS 1,33).

3 Mentioned in § P14 (=YS 2,30).

§ E6 अहिंसाप्रतिष्ठायां तत्संनिधौ वैरत्यागः ।
= YS 2,35 *ahiṃsā-pratiṣṭhāyāṃ tat-saṃnidhau vaira-tyāgaḥ.*

On the basis of non-violence [arises] in his vicinity the renouncement of hostility.

tat-saṃnidhau, 'in his vicinity,' viz. in the vicinity of the yogī. It can also mean 'in the vicinity of practised non-violence.'

§ E7 सत्यप्रतिष्ठायां क्रियाफलाश्रयत्वम् ।
= YS 2,36 *satya-pratiṣṭhāyāṃ kriyā-phalāśrayatvam.*

On the basis of truthfulness there is a connection between action (*kriyā*) and fruit (*phala*).

This is a reference to the doctrine of karma. Karma means 'deed,' the 'fruits' are its consequences. The term 'karma' was transformed here in this sūtra in *kriyā* to make it fit in the context. The words 'karma' and *kriyā* stem from the same verbal root √*kṛ*, 'to do.'

§ E8 अस्तेयप्रतिष्ठायां सर्वरत्नोपस्थानम् ।
= YS 2,37 *asteya-pratiṣṭhāyāṃ sarva-ratnôpasthānam.*

On the basis of 'not stealing' all jewels assemble.

This proverbial saying makes use of a paradox. It is also a fine example of the figure of speech which the Sanskrit poetology, the Alaṃkāraśāstra, calls *atiśaya*, 'exaggeration.' It is similar to the mantra *prātibhād... sarvam*, 'enlightenment brings everything.'[4]

§ E9 ब्रह्मचर्यप्रतिष्ठायां वीर्यलाभः ।
= YS 2,38 *brahmacarya-pratiṣṭhāyāṃ vīrya-lābhaḥ.*

On the basis of chastity one gains energy (or: potency).

vīrya is not only 'energy', but especially 'potency' and 'semen' („mannliche Kraft, so vor allem: männlicher Same“, pw).

The sage Vibhāṇḍaka is an illustrious and illustrative example that potency (*vīrya*) is gained by chastity (*brahmacarya*). The great Sanskrit epic *Mahābhārata* describes him as one who 'completely consisted of penance,' whose soul was 'plain chastity,' and, in the next word, he is called by the epithet 'having fruitful or productive

4 § C26 (=YS 3,34).

potency.'[5] The hermit, chaste and potent, makes an antelope pregnant with a human son called Ṛṣyaśṛṅga ('Antelope Horn') who is born with an antelope horn on his forehead.

§ E10 = YS 2,39

अपरिग्रहप्रतिष्ठायां जन्मकथंतासंबोधः ।

aparigraha-sthairye janma-kathaṃtā-saṃbodhaḥ.

On the basis of 'not clinging' [to rebirth arises] enlightenment concerning the circumstances of birth.

Having completed the treatment of the five moral prohibitions, the meditation technique, 'creation of the opposite' (*pratipakṣa-bhāvana*) will now[6] be exerted on the five moral precepts (*niyama*):[7]

§ E11 = YS 2,40

शौचात्स्वाङ्गजुगुप्सा परैरसंसर्गः ।

śaucāt svâṅga-jugupsā parair asaṃsargaḥ.

Out of purity [arises] aversion to one's own body and avoiding of contact with others.

§ E12 = YS 2,41

सत्त्वशुद्धिसौमनस्यैकाग्र्येन्द्रियजयात्मदर्शनयोग्यत्वानि च ।

sattva-śuddhi-saumanasyaikāgryêndriya-jayâtma-darśana-yogyatvāni ca.

[Out of purity, *śauca*, arise] moreover the abilities for benevolence, purity (*śuddhi*), wellbeing, 'one-pointedness' [of the thinking], victory over the sense organs and of seeing the self (*ātman*).

Benevolence (*sattva*) refers to one of the three qualities of matter (*guṇa*).[8]

The activities of the five organs of sense are: hearing (*śrāvaṇa*), sensing (*vedanā*), seeing (*ādarśa*), tasting (*āsvāda*) and smelling (*vārttā*).[9]

'Seeing the self' (*ātma-darśana*), is a reference to the monistic Vedântic concept of *ātman*, the soul. In a secular context, one would understand 'self-awareness.'

5 *tapasā bhāvitâtmanaḥ amogha-vīryasya*, 3.110.11. *The Mahābhārata*. Poona 1942, vol. 3, p. 368-381. English trsl.: *The Mahābhārata*. J. A. B. van Buitenen. (Vol. II, 1975), pp. 431-441. German: *Mahābhārata. Die Großen Erzählungen von den Bhārata*. Trsl. Georg von Simson. Berlin 2011, pp. 129-140.

6 § E11-16 (=YS 2,40-45).

7 The following sūtras comment *niyama*, which contained only two constituents in Patañjali's original § P16 (=YS 2,32), but was enlarged up to five in § E1.

8 § E29 (=YS 1,16), § B24 (=YS 2,15) and § P3 (=YS 2,19).

9 Enumerated in § C29 (= YS 3,37).

§ E13
= YS 2,42

संतोषादनुत्तमः सुखलाभः ।
saṃtoṣād anuttamaḥ sukha-lābhaḥ.

Out of satisfaction [arises] unsurpassable acquisition of happiness.

Or, to quote the German Schopenhauerian Wilhelm Busch, „Ach!“ – spricht er – „die größte Freud'/ Ist doch die Zufriedenheit!!!“[10]

§ E14
= YS 2,43

कायेन्द्रियसिद्धिरशुद्धिक्षयात्तपसः ।
kāyendriya-siddhir aśuddhi-kṣayāt tapasaḥ.

Perfection of the body and the sense organs [arises], because impurity disappears, out of penance.

§ E15
= YS 2,44

स्वाध्यायादिष्टदेवतासंप्रयोगः ।
svâdhyāyād iṣṭa-devatā-saṃprayogaḥ.

By private studies [there is] union with the favourite deity.

'Private studies (*svâdhyāya*) are traditional studies of the Veda.[11]

§ E16
= YS 2,45

समाधिसिद्धिरीश्वरप्रणिधानात् ।
samādhi-siddhir īśvara-praṇidhānāt.

Perfection of 'concentration' (*samādhi*) [is achieved] by devotion to the god.

§ E17-22 Postscript to the Shutdown
(YS 1,17-22)

§ E17
= YS 1,17

वितर्कविचारानन्दास्मितानुगमात्संप्रज्ञातः ।
vitarka-vicārânandâsmitânugamāt saṃprajñātaḥ.

[The shutdown of the movements of thinking] comes after calculating and reflection, bliss and egocentricity. Therefore it is conscious.

One has to add *nirodhaḥ* as the missing subject of *saṃprajñātaḥ*. I have expressed my doubts concerning the authenticity of this sūtra and the whole section E17-22 in the chapter on textual criticism (see p. 23).

10 The famous German humourist, poet and cartoonist (1832-1908), in his most popular classic 'Max und Moritz' (*Wilhelm Busch. Gesamtausgabe in vier Bänden.* Ed. Friedrich Bohne. Wiesbaden, no date, vol. I, p. 365).

11 *svâdhyāya*, the 'private studies' have already appeared in § E2 (=YS 2,1).

§ E18 विरामप्रत्ययाभ्यासपूर्वः संस्कारशेषोऽन्यः ।
= YS 1,18 *virāma-pratyayâbhyāsa-pūrvaḥ saṃskāra-śeṣo 'nyaḥ.*

Previous to the other [kind of shutdown of the movements of thinking, the one that is unconscious] is the exercise of the concept of 'stop' (*virāma*). [This kind of shutdown still] has a remnant of [subconscious karmic] 'imprints' (*saṃskāra*).

What is meant by the exercise of the concept of 'stop' or halt is unclear. Perhaps some kind of meditation technique?

§ E19 भवप्रत्ययो विदेहप्रकृतिलयानाम् ।
= YS 1,19 *bhava-pratyayo videha-prakṛti-layānām.*

[There is] a concept of rebirth of those (souls) who are immaterially dissolved in the matter (*prakṛti*).

'Dissolved in the matter,' because of the remnants of [subconscious karmic] 'imprints' mentioned in the previous sūtra. It is them which cause the next rebirth. Similarly, it is said in the miscellanies (Part D)[12] that the transformation into birth emerges from the abundance of the 'matter' (*prakṛty-āpūrāt*).

bhava, lit. 'becoming,' 'emerging,' is used here in the sense of 'rebirth.'

As to the immaterialness (*videha*), cf. the 'great immaterialisation' (*mahā-videhā*).[13]

§ E20 श्रद्धावीर्यस्मृतिसमाधिप्रज्ञापूर्वक इतरेषाम् ।
= YS 1,20 *śraddhā-vīrya-smṛti-samādhi-prajñā-pūrvaka itareṣām.*

As to the others[14] (viz. the individual 'souls' which are already reborn), there is confidence, energy, mindfulness, 'concentration' and insight [as preconditions] prior [to the shutdown of the movements of thinking].

The yogī acquires energy (*vīrya*) by meditation on chasteness.[15]

12 § D1 (=YS 4,2).

13 In § C36 (=YS 3,44).

14 Concerning the usage of *itara*, also in § C9 (=YS 3,17) and § D6 (=YS 4,7), cf. *itaratra* in § B4 (=YS 1,4) and *anya* in § E18 (=YS 1,18), § E38-39 (=YS 1,49-50) and § P6 (=YS 2,22).

15 According to § E9 (=YS 2,38).

§ E21 तीव्रसंवेगानामासन्नः ।
= YS 1,21 *tīvra-saṃvegānām āsannaḥ.*

For those of acute impetuousness, it (viz. the shutdown of the movements of thinking) is near.

For textual criticism of this and the next sūtra, see again p. 23f.

§ E22 मृदुमध्याधिमात्रत्वात् ततोऽपि विशेषः ।
= YS 1,22 *mṛdu-madhyâdhimātratvāt tato 'pi viśeṣaḥ.*

But from the point of view of mildness, mediocrity and exorbitance, there is a difference.

§ E23-28 Shutdown (*nirodha)* by Devotion to the God
(YS 1,23-28)

§ E23 ईश्वरप्रणिधानाद्वा ।
= YS 1,23 *īśvara-praṇidhānād vā.*

Or by devotion to the god (*īśvara-praṇidhāna*) [the shutdown of the movements of the thinking can be achieved].

For textual criticism, see p. 24.

§ E24 क्लेशकर्मविपाकाशयैरपरामृष्टः पुरुषविशेष ईश्वरः ।
= YS 1,24 *kleśa-karma-vipākâśayair aparāmṛṣṭaḥ puruṣa-viśeṣa īśvaraḥ.*

The god (*īśvara*) is a special 'soul' (*puruṣa*), which is untouched by the dispositions (*āśaya*) of the maturation of defiling deeds.

The karma dispositions (*āśaya*) are defined as follows: 'The root of the 'defilements' is a karma disposition (*āśaya*), of which one can make oneself aware concerning the current and non-current rebirths.'[16] *kleśa-karman* deals with the 'cessation of the defiling karma.'[17]

§ E25 तत्र निरतिशयं सर्वज्ञबीजम् ।
= YS 1,25 *tatra niratiśayaṃ sarva-jña-bījam.*

There (in the god, Īśvara) lies the seed of omniscience because he does not have any overlying strata (i.e. covers of karma).

16 § B21 (=YS 2,12).

17 § D29 (=YS 4,30).

This is a commentary on the previous paragraph. The god, Īśvara, is one of the reborn 'souls' (*puruṣa*) which were mentioned in § E20 (=YS 1,20).

§ E26 स पूर्वेषामपि गुरुः कालेनानवच्छेदात् ।
= YS 1,26 *sa pūrveṣām api guruḥ kālenânavacchedāt.*

He was the teacher of the ancients too, owing to his timelessness.

anavaccheda, lit. 'the state of not being cut or trimmed' [by time].

§ E27 तस्य वाचकः प्रणवः ।
= YS 1,27 *tasya vācakaḥ praṇavaḥ.*

His phonetic expression is the syllable *om*.

§ E28 तज्जपस्तदर्थभावनम् ।
= YS 1,28 *taj-japas tad-artha-bhāvanam.*

To mutter it (viz. the syllable *om*) is the meditative creation of its (or his, the god's) meaning.

Dispassion Supreme

§ E29-30 (=YS 1,16-17)

§ E29 तत्परं पुरुषख्यातेर्गुणवैतृष्ण्यम् ।
= YS 1,16 *tat-paraṃ puruṣa-khyāter guṇa-vaitṛṣṇyam.*

Its highest extreme (i.e. the supreme kind of dispassion) is the exemption from thirst after the [three] qualities of 'matter,' of one who realises [the existence of] the *puruṣa* (the individual 'soul').

See notes on p. 25.

§ E30 परमाणुपरममहत्त्वान्तोऽस्य वशीकारः ।
= YS 1,40 *paramâṇu-parama-mahattvânto 'sya vaśīkāraḥ.*

His (he who has mastered 'exercising' and 'dispassion') self-discipline (*vaśīkāra*) ends in the smallest and greatest.

'His' (*asya*), refers to the yogī who has mastered 'exercising' and 'dispassion.' He 'does not thirst after objects' (*viṣaya-vitṛṣṇasya*) and 'realises the individual soul' (*puruṣa-khyāteḥ*). His omnipotence enables him to realise the enlightenment. The ancient Indian poetologists called the figure of speech used here *atiśaya*, 'exaggeration.'

Perhaps there is also a connection with the supernatural faculties (*siddhi*). 'Diminutiveness' (*aṇi-man*)[18] is a formation of the same word as *parama-aṇu*, 'smallest.'

§ E31-40 Additions to the Unification
(YS 1,42-51)

§ E31
= YS 1,42

तत्र शब्दार्थज्ञानविकल्पैः संकीर्णा सवितर्का ।

tatra śabdârtha-jñāna-vikalpaiḥ saṃkīrṇā savitarkā.

That kind of 'unification' which is endowed with calculating (*savitarka*)[19] is mixed with imaginations concerned with the perception of the meaning of words.

tatra, 'there,' during the 'unification' (*samāpatti*).

It has been stated already[20] that imagination (*vikalpa*) is concerned with 'the perception of words.' Here, it is further elaborated by 'the perception of the meaning of words.' It is made clear that the focus lies not only on the formal aspects of speech, but also on its content.

§ E32
= YS 1,43

स्मृतिपरिशुद्धौ स्वरूपशून्येवार्थमात्रनिर्भासा निर्वितर्का ।

smṛti-pariśuddhau sva-rūpa-śūnyêvârtha-mātra-nirbhāsā nirvitarkā.

[During the other kind of 'unification' which is] not endowed with calculating (*nirvitarka*), only the 'sense' (*artha*) radiates, which is, as it were, devoid of that which has the shape (*rūpa*) of the matter (*sva*), after the purification by [the meditative technique of] mindfulness.

sva-rūpa is that which has the shape (*rūpa*) of the matter (*sva*), i.e. the thoughts.[21]

We notice yet another Buddhist influence here. On the fourth and final level of the Buddhist meditation technique of *dhyāna*, the thinking is purified by mindfulness (*smṛti-pariśuddhi*, and also by equanimity, *upekṣā*).[22]

18 *aṇiman*, § C38 (=YS 3,46).

19 *vitarka*, cf. § E17 (=YS 1,17) and § E4 (=YS 2,33).

20 In § B9 (=YS 1,9).

21 See § B3 (=YS 1,3).

22 See the author's article *Meditation (dhyāna) in der ältesten buddhistischen Lehre*, 1990.

§ E33 एतयैव सविचारा निर्विचारा च सूक्ष्मविषया व्याख्याता ।
= YS 1,44 *etayâiva savicārā nirvicārā ca sūkṣma-viṣayā vyākhyātā.*

Thereby[23] [that kind of] 'unification' which is either endowed or not endowed with reflection on subtle (immaterial) objects, is also already explained.

Our sūtra implies that the paragraphs § E31-32 deal with 'coarse' (*sthūla*, i.e. material) objects. What has been said about *savitarkā/nirvitarkā samāpatti* in § E31-32 is – *mutatis mutandis* – valid for *savicārā/nirvicārā samāpatti* here.

§ E34 सूक्ष्मविषयत्वं चालिङ्गपर्यवसानम् ।
= YS 1,45 *sūkṣma-viṣayatvaṃ câliṅga-paryavasānam.*

And the realm of subtle objects finds its termination in the absence of marks (*aliṅga*).

§ E35 ता एव सबीजः समाधिः ।
= YS 1,46 *tā eva sabījaḥ samādhiḥ.*

These (kinds of 'unification,' *samāpatti*) are already the 'concentration with seed.'

For text-critical remarks on this paragraph, see p. 26.

§ E36 निर्विचारवैशारद्येऽध्यात्मप्रसादः ।
= YS 1,47 *nirvicāra-vaiśāradye 'dhyātma-prasādaḥ.*

In that state of maturity[24] which is not endowed with reflection, the clarity pertaining to the *ātman* [sets in].

As to the term *prasāda*, one wonders whether there might be any connection with the exercises called *citta-prasādana.*[25]

§ E37 ऋतंभरा तत्र प्रज्ञा ।
= YS 1,48 *ṛtaṃ-bharā tatra prajñā.*

There (during the 'unification,' *samāpatti*), insight bears the 'truth' (*ṛta*).

23 *etayâiva*, 'thereby,' viz. by § E31-32 (=YS 1,42-43).

24 Cf. § E33 (=YS 1,44).

25 In § B32-39 (=YS 1,32-39).

On *ṛta* and the Vedic world-view, see p. 26.

§ E38
= YS 1,49

श्रुतानुमानप्रज्ञाभ्यामन्यविषया विशेषार्थत्वात् ।
śrutânumāna-prajñābhyām anya-viṣayā viśeṣārthatvāt.

[This insight] has other objects than those two kinds of insight which are based on 'that which was heard (by revelation, i.e. the Veda)' (*śruta*) and on inference, because it is directed towards a special meaning (i.e. the *ṛta*).

śruta: 'that which was heard by revelation, i.e. the Veda, holy learning, sacred knowledge' is Apte's translation, but he adds, 'learning in general.' It looks like *śruta* refers to the sacred knowledge and 'inference' (*anumāna*) to learning in general. *śruta* designates what belongs to the *śruti* tradition, viz. the Veda, or the sacred tradition (*āgama*), respectively.[26]

§ E39
= YS 1,50

तज्जः संस्कारोऽन्यसंस्कारप्रतिबन्धी ।
taj-jaḥ saṃskāro 'nya-saṃskāra-pratibandhī.

The [subconscious karmic] 'imprint' (*saṃskāra*)[27] that is born out of this (kind of insight, viz. out of the *ṛta*) is characterised by its other binding 'imprints.'

§ E40
= YS 1,51

तस्यापि निरोधे सर्वनिरोधान्निर्बीजः समाधिः ।
tasyâpi nirodhe sarva-nirodhān nirbījaḥ samādhiḥ.

After this [kind of karmic 'imprint'] has been shut down too, because [now] everything is shut down, the 'seedless concentration'[28] [sets in].

§ E41 Birth, Drugs, Mantras, Austerities and Concentration
(=YS 4,1)

§ E41
= YS 4,1

जन्मौषधिमन्त्रतपःसमाधिजाः सिद्धयः ।
janmauṣadhi-mantra-tapaḥ-samādhi-jāḥ siddhayaḥ.

The supernatural faculties (*siddhi*) are born from birth, drugs, mantras, austerities and 'concentration' (*samādhi*).

26 *āgama*, § B7 (=YS 1,7). Cf. also *anuśravika* in § B27 (=YS 1,13).

27 *saṃskāra*, § E18f (=YS 1,18f) passim, esp. § C1 (=YS 3,9).

28 Cf. § C05 (=YS 3,8).

See p. 26. This model of an interpolation seems like a befitting conclusion for the 'extras' of the Yogasūtras.

Postscript

Yoga and Its Position in Hindu Philosophy

In the elder Upaniṣad literature, at the beginnings of Indian philosophy (about 800-600 BC), two ideas emerge side by side. They were bound to become determinant for the history of Indian religions:

- the doctrine of karma, and
- the assumption of universal suffering.

From the combination of both concepts, follows: all is suffering, and all suffering is self-inflicted.

Karma means 'deed.' The doctrine of karma says that every action has a reaction, a fruit, which falls back upon the actor. Each maturation corresponds exactly to the deed by which it was caused. Under the principle of karma, gods become superfluous, because man creates his fate himself, by his deeds. 'One becomes good by good deeds and evil by evil deeds,' declares the Bṛhadāraṇyaka-Upaniṣad (3,2,13).

The law of karma is closely connected with the belief in the cycle of reincarnation, the saṃsāra. According to this conception, world affairs procede cyclically. There is no beginning and no end. After death, the soul seeks a new body in a stone, a plant, an animal, a human or superhuman being. 'As man removes worn-out clothes and dons others, new ones, in the same way the soul removes the worn-out bodies and enters others, new ones.' (Bhagavadgītā 2,22) The kind of rebirth is determined by one's deeds, the karma. 'Those who have here a decent conduct can expect to attain a decent womb. Those, however, who have an indecent conduct can expect to attain an indecent womb, that of a bitch, a sow or a woman of the most ignoble caste (*caṇḍālā*).' (Chāndogya-Upaniṣad 5,10,7)

One might think that the belief in transmigration robs death of its horrors. In the cycle of rebirths, death is not a final conclusion, nor has one to await eternal damnation in hell or bliss in paradise. Instead, one can figure out how good or bad the next incarnation will be. But the problem shifts: in the cycle of reincarnations, the absolute evil is not death, but the compulsive return, the must-live. That you are ensnared in the cycle at all, the fact that you exist, the plain 'being' is experienced as suffering. This suffering rouses the wish not to be reborn, a craving for renunciation, for the deliverance from universal suffering. The Bṛhadāraṇyaka-Upaniṣad (3.4) says:

> 'What lies beyond hunger and thirst, sorrow, error, old age and death, there the brahmins see the self. They give up the desire for children, the desire for property, the desire for the world and walk away as beggars. The desire for sons is a desire for property, the desire for property is a desire for the world. Both are desire. That is why a scholar, having become weary of scholarship,

shall abide in simplicity. Having become weary of simplicity as well as of scholarship, he becomes a silent hermit. Having become weary of silence as well as of non-silence, he becomes a genuine brahmin – *anything else is suffering.*'

Here, the conviction of the universal suffering in the cycle of reincarnation is enunciated for the first time.

We find the same notion of the universal suffering again, about half a millennium later, in the Yogasūtras, where it reads, '*All is only suffering* for a discriminator.' (*duḥkham eva sarvaṃ vivekinaḥ*, § B24=YS 2,15).

Elder Upaniṣads	~ 800-600 BC
Bṛhadāraṇyaka-Upaniṣad	
Chāndogya-Upaniṣad	
Buddha	6th century
Aśoka	
universal monarch	3rd cent.
Patañjali	
and the Yogasūtras	2nd cent. BC
Vyāsa	
and his commentary	~ 500 AD

The Yogasūtras of Patañjali are the main text of the yoga philosophy. The otherwise unknown author[1] dates from the second century BC. The words 'yoga' and 'yoke' are etymologically and semantically related. Yoga means 'to yoke,' like: to yoke an ox. What is meant is: to yoke the mind, in order to direct it towards deliverance.

Yoga is the most ancient of the six philosophical systems into which Indian philosophy is traditionally divided, viz. the six darśanas or 'views.' These six philosophical schools can be grouped in three pairs, the first of which explains the world in a *pluralistic* approach, the second *dualistic* and the third *monistic*.

• The first pair which assumes a *plurality* of the categories of being are Nyāya and Vaiśeṣika. (1) Nyāya, or logic, is ascribed to its founder Gautama.[2] (2) Vaiśeṣika, the 'doctrine of the differences,' to Kaṇāda.

• *Dualistic* are the (3) Sāṃkhya of Īśvarakṛṣṇa and the (4) Yoga of Patañjali.

• *Monistic* models of world-explanation offer the (5) Mīmāṃsā of Jaimini which is based on Vedic ritualism and the (6) Vedānta of Bādarāyaṇa.

Sāṃkhya and Yoga (nos. 3 and 4), the *dualistic* proposals, are most closely related to each other. They can be understood as two aspects of the same philosophy. Sāṃ-

1 To identify him with the famous grammarian Patañjali is unfounded speculation.

2 Not to be confused with the Buddha who had the same family name.

khya is the theory, Yoga the practice. Sāṃkhya provides the theoretical superstructure, yoga teaches the practical methods.

Spiritual yoga is a way – not of living, but *out of* life. The yogic method claims to be a path to redemption from the suffering in the cycle of rebirth. In the west, philosophy and religion are two different concepts. To say it in the simplest way, philosophy is concerned with thinking, religion with faith. It is different with Hindu *philosophy* and Hindu *religion*: they cannot be keenly kept apart from each other because not only Hindu religion, but Hindu philosophy, too, always has a practical reference to salvation.

Glossary of Frequent Terms

āśaya, a subconscious karma disposition. (§ B21 = YS 2,12). → *saṃskāra*.
dharmāḥ (*dharma* in the plural), 'entity factors'; the Buddhist meaning of (Pāli) *dhamma* (in the pl.) is 'an essential attribute of men and animals; a quality or characteristic' (M. Cone: *Dict. of Pāli*, II, p. 461).
dhyāna, 'meditation'; 'What ... has only one thread of concept is meditation.' (§ P28 = YS 3,2)
dṛśya, a term for the → matter.
guṇa, 'quality,' (§ P3) 'attribute'; according to the classical system of the Sāṃkhya philosopy, the three qualities (*guṇa*) of the 'matter' are benevolence (*sattva*), passion (*rajas*) and darkness (*tamas*). Of the three, only benevolence occurs in the Yogasūtras.
kleśa, 'defilements'; (1) Ignorance, (2) egocentricity, (3) passion, (4) hate and (5) zest for life are the 'defilements.' (§ B12 = YS 2,3)
matter, also termed *sva* or *dṛśya*. Its attributes are enumerated in § P2-3. The matter is one of the two fundamental categories of being. The other is the → soul.
pariṇāma, 'transformation'; of *nirodha*, *samādhi* and *ekâgratā*, shall enable the yogī to perform the siddhis. (§ C1-7 = YS 3,9-15)
prakṛti, the 'matter'; the opposite of the 'soul' (*puruṣa*). (§ E19 =YS 1,19) and § D1 = YS 4,2).
pratyaya, 'concept,' an object of meditation beyond logical thinking. For example, the soul observes by means of *pratyaya*. (§ P4) The term is used ten times altogether in the Yogasūtras, twice by Patañjali, and also by all his epigones in Parts B-E.
samādhi, 'concentration'; the final state of meditation, the endpoint of the eightfold path. '...when only the object is radiating and when it is devoid of the matter.' (§ P29 = YS 3,3).
saṃskāra, a subconscious karma imprint; the saṃskāras are responsible for a person acting similarly over and over again in similar situations, collecting ever new karma, and being therefore reincarnated. → *āśaya*.
saṃyama, 'interconnection'; of the three → *pariṇāma*, a method of how to perform certain siddhis. (§ C8 = YS 3,16)
siddhi, 'supernatural faculty.'
smṛti, 'mindfulness'; 'If one does not let the objects be stolen which one has sensed, [this] is mindfulness.' (§ B11= YS 1,11).
soul, also termed the 'lord' (*svāmin*), or the 'observer' (*draṣṭṛ*). The soul is pure 'observing.' (§ P4 = YS 2,20) The soul is one of the two fundamental categories of being. The other is the → matter. As to the philosophical term 'soul' (*puruṣa*) in the post-Patañjali parts of the Yogasūtras, see notes on § B3 (p. 45).

sva, a term for the → matter.
vṛtti, 'movement' of the thinking, brain movement. (§ B6-11 = YS 1,6-11).

Sūtra, Paragraph and Page Number in the Order of the Vulgate

YS	*§*	*Page*
1,1 =	§ B1	p. 30
1,2 =	§ B2	p. 44
1,3 =	§ B3	p. 45
1,4 =	§ B4	p. 46
1,5 =	§ B5	p. 46
1,6 =	§ B6	p. 47
1,7 =	§ B7	p. 47
1,8 =	§ B8	p. 47
1,9 =	§ B9	p. 47
1,10 =	§ B10	p. 48
1,11 =	§ B11	p. 48
1,12 =	§ B26	p. 53
1,13 =	§ B27	p. 54
1,14 =	§ B28	p. 54
1,15 =	§ B40	p. 59
1,16 =	§ E29	p. 96
1,17 =	§ E17	p. 93
1,18 =	§ E18	p. 94
1,19 =	§ E19	p. 94
1,20 =	§ E20	p. 94
1,21 =	§ E21	p. 95
1,22 =	§ E22	p. 95
1,23 =	§ E23	p. 95
1,24 =	§ E24	p. 95
1,25 =	§ E25	p. 95
1,26 =	§ E26	p. 96
1,27 =	§ E27	p. 96
1,28 =	§ E28	p. 96
1,29 =	§ B29	p. 55
1,30 =	§ B30	p. 55
1,31 =	§ B31	p. 55
1,32 =	§ B32	p. 56
1,33 =	§ B33	p. 57
1,34 =	§ B34	p. 57
1,35 =	§ B35	p. 57
1,36 =	§ B36	p. 58
1,37 =	§ B37	p. 58
1,38 =	§ B38	p. 58
1,39 =	§ B39	p. 58
1,40 =	§ E30	p. 96
1,41 =	§ B41	p. 59
1,42 =	§ E31	p. 97
1,43 =	§ E32	p. 97
1,44 =	§ E33	p. 98
1,45 =	§ E34	p. 98
1,46 =	§ E35	p. 98
1,47 =	§ E36	p. 98
1,48 =	§ E37	p. 98
1,49 =	§ E38	p. 99
1,50 =	§ E39	p. 99
1,51 =	§ E40	p. 99
2,1 =	§ E2	p. 89
2,2 =	§ E3	p. 90
2,3 =	§ B12	p. 48
2,4 =	§ B13	p. 49
2,5 =	§ B14	p. 49
2,6 =	§ B15	p. 49
2,7 =	§ B16	p. 50
2,8 =	§ B17	p. 50
2,9 =	§ B18	p. 51
2,10 =	§ B19	p. 51
2,11 =	§ B20	p. 51
2,12 =	§ B21	p. 52
2,13 =	§ B22	p. 37
2,14 =	§ B23	p. 52
2,15 =	§ B24	p. 52
2,16 =	§ B25	p. 53
2,17 =	§ P1	p. 31
2,18 =	§ P2	p. 32
2,19 =	§ P3	p. 32
2,20 =	§ P4	p. 33
2,21 =	§ P5	p. 33
2,22 =	§ P6	p. 34
2,23 =	§ P7	p. 35
2,24 =	§ P8	p. 35
2,25 =	§ P9	p. 35
2,26 =	§ P10	p. 36
2,27 =	§ P11	p. 36
2,28 =	§ P12	p. 37
2,29 =	§ P13	p. 37
2,30 =	§ P14	p. 37
2,31 =	§ P15	p. 38
2,32 =	§ P16	p. 39
and =	§ E1	p. 89
2,33 =	§ E4	p. 90
2,34 =	§ E5	p. 90
2,35 =	§ E6	p. 91
2,36 =	§ E7	p. 91
2,37 =	§ E8	p. 91
2,38 =	§ E9	p. 91
2,39 =	§ E10	p. 92
2,40 =	§ E11	p. 92
2,41 =	§ E12	p. 92
2,42 =	§ E13	p. 93
2,43 =	§ E14	p. 93
2,44 =	§ E15	p. 93
2,45 =	§ E16	p. 93
2,46 =	§ P17	p. 39
2,47 =	§ P18	p. 39
2,48 =	§ P19	p. 39
2,49 =	§ P20	p. 39
2,50 =	§ P21	p. 40
2,51 =	§ P22	p. 40
2,52 =	§ P23	p. 40
2,53 =	§ P24	p. 40
2,54 =	§ P25	p. 41
2,55 =	§ P26	p. 41
3,1 =	§ P27	p. 41
3,2 =	§ P28	p. 42
3,3 =	§ P29	p. 43

YS	*§*	*Page*
3,4 =	§ C01	p. 63
3,5 =	§ C02	p. 63
3,6 =	§ C03	p. 63
3,7 =	§ C04	p. 64
3,8 =	§ C05	p. 64
3,9 =	§ C1	p. 64
3,10 =	§ C2	p. 65
3,11 =	§ C3	p. 65
3,12 =	§ C4	p. 66
3,13 =	§ C5	p. 66
3,14 =	§ C6	p. 66
3,15 =	§ C7	p. 67
3,16 =	§ C8	p. 67
3,17 =	§ C9	p. 67
3,18 =	§ C10	p. 68
3,19 =	§ C11	p. 68
3,20 =	§ C12	p. 68
3,21 =	§ C13	p. 69
3,22 =	§ C14	p. 69
3,23 =	§ C15	p. 69
3,24 =	§ C16	p. 70
3,25 =	§ C17	p. 70
3,26 =	§ C18	p. 70
3,27 =	§ C19	p. 71
3,28 =	§ C20	p. 71
3,29 =	§ C21	p. 71
3,30 =	§ C22	p. 71
3,31 =	§ C23	p. 72
3,32 =	§ C24	p. 72
3,33 =	§ C25	p. 72
3,34 =	§ C26	p. 72
3,35 =	§ C27	p. 72
3,36 =	§ C28	p. 73
3,37 =	§ C29	p. 73
3,38 =	§ C30	p. 73
3,39 =	§ C31	p. 74
3,40 =	§ C32	p. 74
3,41 =	§ C33	p. 74
3,42 =	§ C34	p. 75
3,43 =	§ C35	p. 75
3,44 =	§ C36	p. 75
3,45 =	§ C37	p. 76
3,46 =	§ C38	p. 76
3,47 =	§ C39	p. 76
3,48 =	§ C40	p. 77
3,49 =	§ C41	p. 77
3,50 =	§ C42	p. 78
3,51 =	§ C43	p. 78
3,52 =	§ C44	p. 78
3,53 =	§ C45	p. 79
3,54 =	§ C46	p. 79
3,55 =	§ C47	p. 79
3,56 =	§ C48	p. 79
4,1 =	§ E41	p. 99
4,2 =	§ D1	p. 80
4,3 =	§ D2	p. 80
4,4 =	§ D3	p. 81
4,5 =	§ D4	p. 81
4,6 =	§ D5	p. 81
4,7 =	§ D6	p. 81
4,8 =	§ D7	p. 82
4,9 =	§ D8	p. 82
4,10 =	§ D9	p. 82
4,11 =	§ D10	p. 82
4,12 =	§ D11	p. 83
4,13 =	§ D12	p. 83
4,14 =	§ D13	p. 83
4,15 =	§ D14	p. 83
4,16 =	§ D15	p. 84
4,17 =	§ D16	p. 84
4,18 =	§ D17	p. 84
4,19 =	§ D18	p. 84
4,20 =	§ D19	p. 85
4,21 =	§ D20	p. 85
4,22 =	§ D21	p. 86
4,23 =	§ D22	p. 86
4,24 =	§ D23	p. 86
4,25 =	§ D24	p. 86
4,26 =	§ D25	p. 87
4,27 =	§ D26	p. 87
4,28 =	§ D27	p. 87
4,29 =	§ D28	p. 87
4,30 =	§ D29	p. 87
4,31 =	§ D30	p. 87
4,32 =	§ D31	p. 88
4,33 =	§ D32	p. 88
4,34 =	§ D33	p. 88

Abbreviations and Bibliography

Apte = Apte, Vaman Shivaram: *The Practical Sanskrit-English Dictionary*. Revised and Enlarged Edition. Reprinted Kyoto 1978.

B = Bangali Baba: *Yogasūtra of Patañjali*. With the Commentary of Vyāsa, trsl. from Sanskrit into English. Ed. and trsl. Delhi 1976.

BHSD = Edgerton, Franklin: *Buddhist Hybrid Sanskrit Grammar and Dictionary*, Vol. II: *Dictionary*. 1977 ([1]1952).

Cone, Margaret: *A Dictionary of Pāli*. Oxford 2001-.

(A) Critical Pāli Dictionary, (*a-kāreti*) begun by Vilhelm Trenckner... . Copenhagen 1924-Bristol 2011.

Deussen, Paul: *Allgemeine Geschichte der Philosophie*. I, 3 (Second ed.) Leipzig 1914, pp. 511ff.

Frauwallner, Erich: [the chapter:] *Das Sāṃkhya und das klassische Yoga-System*. In: *Geschichte der indischen Philosophie*, Bd. 1. Salzburg 1953, pp. 275-450; on the 25 categories of the Sāṃkhya system notably pp. 348-356.

H = Hauer, J. W.: *Der Yoga. Ein indischer Weg zum Selbst*. Stuttgart 1958, pp. 239ff.

Jackmuth, Martina: *Die Bildersprache Kālidāsas im Kumārasaṃbhava*. (Beiträge zur Indologie, vol. 35). Harrassowitz: Wiesbaden 2002.

Lüders, Heinrich: *Varuna*. Aus dem Nachlaß hrsg. v. Ludwig Alsdorf. I: *Varuna und die Wasser*. II: *Varuna und das Rta*. Göttingen 1951, 1959.

Maas, Paul: *Textual Criticism*. Oxford 1967. – [German original:] *Textkritik*. Leipzig (2. Aufl., durchgesehen, erweitert) [2]1950.

Mayrhofer, Manfred: *Etymologisches Wörterbuch des Altindoarischen*. 3 vols. Heidelberg 1992-2001.

Meisig, Konrad: *Yogasūtra-Konkordanz* (Beiträge zur Indologie, 22). Wiesbaden 1988.

– –: *Das Śrāmaṇyaphala-Sūtra. Synoptische Übersetzung und Glossar der chinesischen Fassungen verglichen mit dem Sanskrit und Pāli* (Freiburger Beiträge zur Indologie, vol. 19). Otto Harrassowitz: Wiesbaden 1987.

– –: *Das Sūtra von den vier Ständen. Das Aggañña-Sutta im Licht seiner chinesischen Parallelen* (Freiburger Beiträge zur Indologie, Bd. 20). Otto Harrassowitz: Wiesbaden 1988.

– –: *Meditation (dhyāna) in der ältesten buddhistischen Lehre*. In: Ludwig Hagemann/ Ernst Pulsfort (ed.): „Ihr alle aber seid Brüder", Festschrift für A. Th. Khoury zum 60. Geburtstag (Würzburger Forschungen zur Missions- und Religionswissenschaft, Religionswissenschaftliche Studien 14), Würzburg – Altenberge 1990, pp. 541-554.

– –: *Sheng Tao King. Die chinesische Fassung des Mahācattārīsaka-Sutta.* In: *Hinduismus und Buddhismus – Festschrift für Ulrich Schneider*, hrsg. v. Harry Falk. Freiburg 1987, pp. 220-248.
– –: *On the Precanonical Shape of the Kevaddha-sutta as Compared with the Kien-ku-king.* In: ‚Premier Colloque Étienne Lamotte (Bruxelles et Liège 24-27 septembre 1989),' Publications de l'Institut Orientaliste de Louvain 42. Université Catholique de Louvain, Institut Orientaliste Louvain-La-Neuve, 1993, pp. 63-70.
– –: *Buddhismus und Wunderglaube.* In: Jahrbuch für Religionswissenschaft und Theologie der Religionen, Bd. 1. Herder: Freiburg, 1993, pp. 72-89.
– –: *A Translation of the Chinese Kevaddhasutta. Together with the Critical Apparatus of the Pāli Text.* In: Festschrift Dieter Schlingloff, ed. F. Wilhelm, 1995, pp. 187-200.
– –: *Klang der Stille. Der Buddhismus.* Freiburg, Basel, Wien, ([1]1995) 2003.
– –: *Shivas Tanz. Der Hinduismus.* Freiburg, Basel, Wien, ([1]1996) 2003.
– –: *Wahrheit im Hinduismus.* In: *Jahrbuch für Religionsphilosophie*, vol. 4, 2005, pp. 35-53.
– –: *Beginnings of Buddhist Ethics. The Chinese Parallel to the Kūṭadantasutta.* Edited, translated and compared with the Pāli (East Asia Intercultural Studies – Interkulturelle Ostasienstudien, 4). Harrassowitz: Wiesbaden 2011.
Pali-English Dictionary. Ed. by T. W. Rhys Davids and William Stede. London 1921-1925.
pw = Böhtlingk, O.: *Sanskrit-Wörterbuch in kürzerer Fassung.* 3 Vols. Akademische Druck- u. Verlagsanstalt: Graz 1959.
Schneider, Ulrich: *Die Großen Felsenedikte Aśokas.* Kritische Ausgabe, Übersetzung und Analyse der Texte (Freiburger Beiträge zur Indologe, Bd. 11. Harrassowitz: Wiesbaden 1978.
– –: *Der Buddhismus. Eine Einführung.* Wissenschaftliche Buchgesellschaft: Darmstadt [4]1997 ([1]1980).
– –: *Einführung in den Hinduismus.* Wissenschaftliche Buchgesellschaft: Darmstadt 1989.
Schreiner, Peter: *Yoga. Grundlagen, Methoden, Ziele. Ein bibliographischer Überblick.* Köln 1979.
Wackernagel, Jakob & Debrunner, Albert: *Altindische Grammatik.* Vols. I-III, Göttingen 1896-1930, Register by Richard Hauschild 1964.
Weinrich, Harald: *Semantik der kühnen Metapher.* In: Anselm Haverkamp (ed.): *Theorie der Metapher.* Darmstadt 1983, p. 316-339. = *Sprache in Texten.* Stuttgart 1976, p. 295-316. Zuerst erschienen in: *Deutsche Vierteljahreszeitschrift*, 37, 1963, p. 325-344.
YS = Yogasūtra(s).
For more abbreviations, especially of the sigla of editions and translations of the YS, see the author's: *Yogasūtra-Konkordanz*, 1988, pp. 55ff.

Beiträge zur Indologie

Herausgegeben von Konrad Meisig

50: Andreas Bock-Raming

Indische Schachspielkunst im 19. Jahrhundert: Triveṅgaḍācāryas Vilāsamaṇimañjarī

Neuedition und annotierte Übersetzung des Sanskrit-Textes

2018. X, 314 Seiten, 95 Abb., br
170x240 mm
ISBN 978-3-447-10965-9
⊙E-Book: ISBN 978-3-447-19729-8 *je € 68,– (D)*

Mit der *Vilāsamaṇimañjarī*, verfasst von dem am Hofe des Marathen-Herrschers Bājī Rāo II. (1775–1851) wirkenden Dichter und Gelehrten Triveṅgaḍācārya, liegt ein weitgehend metrischer Sanskrit-Text vor, der knapp einhundert Schachprobleme und deren Lösungen beschreibt. Andreas Bock-Raming legt nun eine Neuedition und erstmals auch eine deutsche Übersetzung vor, die es erlauben, in größerem Umfang zu dokumentieren, wie in Indien das Regelwerk älterer Schachtexte adaptiert und neu gestaltet wurde.
Eine ausführliche Einleitung bietet einen Überblick über die indischen Primärtexte zum Schach und beschreibt Aufbau, Anlage und Inhalt der Vilāsamaṇimañjarī sowie die Grundlagen der Textedition. Der Sanskrit-Text und dessen Übersetzung werden durch Anmerkungen und Erläuterungen erschlossen, die sowohl inhaltliche als auch lexikalische und grammatische Fragestellungen erörtern. Auf diese Weise leistet der Band einen wesentlichen Beitrag zur Erforschung der literarischen Quellen des indischen Schachspiels.

51: Konrad Meisig

Guttilakāvyaya Der Bodhisattva als Musiker

Singhalesisch – Deutsch
mit Kommentar und einer Sanskrit-Chāyā

2023. 764 Seiten, gb
170x240 mm
ISBN 978-3-447-12005-0
⊙E-Book: ISBN 978-3-447-39390-4 *je € 128,– (D)*

Als Höhepunkt der klassischen singhalesischen Literatur gilt das *Guttilakāvyaya*, das „Gedicht über Guttila", oder freier formuliert das Gedicht über den Buddha in einer früheren Existenz als Musiker Guttila. Das Werk entstand in der Mitte des 15. Jahrhunderts. Es ist eine Bearbeitung des in Pāli, der Kirchensprache des Buddhismus, abgefassten *Guttilajātaka* (Jātaka Nr. 243) und erzählt in insgesamt 511 Versen, wie der Bodhisattva, also der zukünftige Buddha, in einem früheren Leben als Musiker einen undankbaren Schüler in einem Musikerwettstreit besiegt.
Ziel der von Konrad Meisig vorgelegten vollständigen Ausgabe und kommentierten Übersetzung des *Guttilakāvyaya* ist es, erstmals einer westlichen und – mittels der Sanskrit-Chāyā – auch einer gebildeten indischen Leserschaft das Verständnis des in Sri Lanka bis auf den heutigen Tag populären Werks zu ermöglichen – inhaltlich, lexikalisch, grammatikalisch und poetologisch.
Ein Anhang bietet zusätzlich eine Übersetzung des Pāli-*Guttilajātaka*, außerdem einen vollständigen Index der singhalesischen Wörter, eine Zusammenstellung der neu aufgefundenen Etymologien sowie der tamilischen Lehnwörter.

Beiträge zur Indologie

Herausgegeben von Konrad Meisig

52: Konrad Meisig, Marion Meisig

Tamil Temples

Traditional and Transcultural
Thirty-Three Sketches

2024. XX, 388 pages, 637 ill., 1 table, hc
170x240mm
ISBN 978-3-447-12192-7
⊙E-Book: ISBN 978-3-447-39526-7 *each € 89,– (D)*

Since the middle of the 1990s, Tamil migrants have built Śaiva temples. These are based on the pattern of their South Indian and Sri Lankan homelands but with significant modifications, transformations and altered functions resulting from new circumstances and pressures to adapt to the status of an immigrant. Traditionally confined to South Asia, Hinduism is being spread world-wide by modern migration movements. As the world's third largest religious community after Christianity and Islam, Hinduism is currently in the process of developing from a folk religion into a world religion. It is emigrant Hinduism which is primarily responsible for this epochal change. The religious metamorphosis is not taking place in India itself, but overseas. This makes expat-Hinduism an important subject of research for Indologists. The comparison of Hinduism abroad with original Hinduism in India and Sri Lanka enables predictions about possible development opportunities in the home countries.

In their book Konrad and Marion Meisig offer sketches of thirty-three Tamil Śaiva temples in India, Sri Lanka, Germany, Canada, Great Britain and Mauritius. These sketches are based on four categories of temples, depending on whether their principal deity is Gaṇeśa, Muru- gan, a goddess (Devī) or Śiva. There are three methods of presentation: text, picture and ground plan. All three are equally important. This combination will convey the comprehensive religious-historical information.

53: Konrad Meisig (Hg.)

Kālidāsa
Wolkenbote

Metrisch aus dem Sanskrit übertragen
Zweisprachig
Mit Kommentar, Verskonkordanz
der Verschränkungswörter und
vollständigem Sanskritindex

2024. 206 Seiten, 24 Abb., gb
170x240 mm
ISBN 978-3-447-12294-8
⊙E-Book: ISBN 978-3-447-39623-3 *je € 58,– (D)*

Der „Wolkenbote", *Meghadūta*, Höhepunkt der klassischen Sanskritpoesie, kann als eines der schönsten Gedichte der Weltliteratur betrachtet werden. Kālidāsa, der indische Dichterfürst, hat sein Meisterwerk um das Jahr 410 n.Chr. verfasst. Es schildert in 121 Versen, wie ein in Verbannung lebender, vor Trennungsschmerz halb wahnsinniger, aber gutartiger Dämon einem zum Himālaya ziehenden Monsunwolkenturm eine Botschaft für seine geliebte Frau mit auf den Weg gibt.

Der „Wolkenbote" wurde nahezu endlos memoriert, ediert, kommentiert und übersetzt. Konrad Meisigs Übertragung ins Deutsche verfolgt nun gleich mehrere neue Ansätze. Sie wendet sich nicht nur an Indologen, sondern auch an ein breiteres, weltliterarisch interessiertes Lesepublikum. Erstmals bleibt hier das Sanskritmetrum des Originals erhalten. Die beigefügten Materialien bieten – über den allgemeinverständlichen Sachkommentar hinaus – den Sanskrittext in Devanāgarī- und lateinischer Schrift, eine philologische Wort-für-Wort-Übersetzung sowie Vokabelhilfen. Eine Besonderheit des „Wolkenboten" sind die sog. Verschränkungswörter (Schubring), mit denen der Dichter die Reihenfolge der einzelnen Verse markiert hat. Diese Wortklammern sind in einer Verskonkordanz vollständig aufgelistet. Sie beweisen, dass allein der Kommentator Mallinātha (15. Jh.) die von Kālidāsa selbst gewollte Versfolge bewahrt hat. Die erweiterte Literarkritik kommt zu dem Ergebnis, dass Kālidāsa die Verse des „Wolkenboten" überwiegend in Dreiergruppen geformt hat, was die Diskussionsgrundlage um die Echtheit der Strophen weiter stärkt.

Ein vollständiger Index der Sanskritwörter erschließt den Urtext.